WHERE STARS WON'T SHINE

PATRICK LACEY

Grindhouse Press
PO BOX 521
Dayton, Ohio 45401

Grindhouse Press #044
ISBN-10: 1-941918-36-0
ISBN-13: 978-1-941918-36-4

This book is about trauma. If you're dealing with your demons, you're not alone. Your scars are beautiful and so is your persistence. Keep on keeping on.

Other Titles By Patrick Lacey

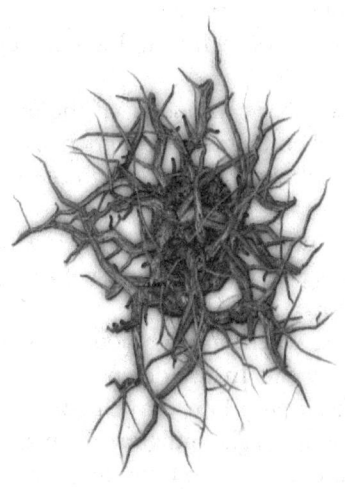

The following is a rejected introduction to Charles Williamson's true crime book *Birth of a Monster.*

EDITOR'S NOTE: *There's some interesting imagery here but it's too personal. Perhaps rework into more factual information or remove altogether. We want to remind people that this is true. It's not a horror novel.*

If you've never heard of Marlowe, Massachusetts, consider yourself lucky. The trees are bare for most of the year, as if winter never truly goes away. The clouds are thick like smog and they rarely let the sun through. Everything is cold. You shiver from the moment you cross the town line until the moment you finally pass through.

There's no reason to visit such a place. A place that is, for lack of a better term, a ghost town. There was a time when Marlowe flourished. At the turn of the century, the mill buildings were fully operational and still open for business. Now, you'd be hard pressed to find a single store with its lights on past four o'clock in the afternoon. That's not to say the town is abandoned. There are those brave souls who chose to stay after the Marlowe Massacre. Take

Betty Packer, for example. A woman old enough to remember the first televisions, yet speaks and jokes like someone a third her age. She's been local for nearly eighty years, living in the same house as her parents and grandparents before her.

"It's my home," she says each time I ask the question that's on everyone's mind.

Why stay in a town that's rotting from the inside out? Why remain in such a place when there are reminders everywhere you look of a man so vile, so ruthless, he's become more of a legend than a killer?

And that's the question I've tried to answer with this book. Perhaps I have or perhaps all I've done is pose more questions. Maybe some questions don't *have* answers.

I can only speculate where the infamous killer of over one hundred innocent people went. In my defense, neither the police nor the detectives who dealt with him can tell you for certain. He was simply there in his cell one night and gone the next morning.

But I can tell you everything leading up to his disappearance. I can tell you about the victims and the families. I can tell you about the trail of bloodshed Tucker Ashton left over much of the country. I can tell you about his childhood and home life, both of which molded him into the monster he became. And that's a term I'll use frequently: monster. You can call him a human if you'd like but you haven't sat across a table and stared into his eyes. You haven't heard him speak of disemboweling little girls like he was recalling a fond memory. You haven't seen his smile when he studies photos of his crime scenes. I hope you never do but if, for some reason, you find yourself in such a position, you'll understand my choice of words.

ONE

THE PHONE RANG. He let it go to voicemail.

"Charles, it's Frank. I know it's early but you never sleep anyway. I just sent you a review that's going to make you salivate. It's *Publishers Weekly*. They said you're the next Harold Schechter, that you've done for Tucker what he did for just about every other serial killer. This is big. Do me a favor, will you? Don't be so bashful. Read the review and give me a call back. You've written a damned good book, a *special* book. It's time to share it with the world."

The message did not end there. Frank Neville, Charles' agent, went on about how they'd be selling a million copies easily. People ate this sort of thing up. There'd been a lull in true crime these last few years, but publishing was cyclical and they'd hit the proverbial sweet spot.

Frank's voice slowly changed, became more distorted. There was nothing wrong with the answering machine. It was a new model, purchased just last month, and the messages usually sounded crystal clear. Charles Williamson didn't own a cell phone. He was a man born years too late, didn't like to be bothered if he could avoid it. After a few moments, the distortion grew to a crescendo. The voice

1

no longer belonged to Frank.

"... and the blood will run like rain, drowning everyone and everything. It will cover the earth until there is nothing but red. And it's all thanks to you, Charles. You made me what I am, after all. You made me a legend. Or a monster if you prefer."

Charles had been hearing the voice more and more, ever since the publisher had set a date for the book, that date being today. He unplugged the answering machine, wrapped the cord around the unit, and tossed it across the room. It shattered against the mantle, several plastic shards spilling to the floor.

The message did not stop.

He was able to block it out for a time, though he knew the relief would not last long. It never did.

It was a strange day for Charles Williamson. He'd waited all his life for this. He ought to be happy. *Birth of a Monster* had taken several years of research and had nearly driven him insane on more than one occasion.

You are *insane,* he thought as he drained the rest of his coffee, which was mostly whiskey.

Or had his inner monologue been the *other* voice, the one that belonged to a serial killer? He couldn't be certain. Some days, they were one in the same.

Now that the book was finally hitting shelves, happiness was no longer in his vocabulary. Not after what he'd seen and witnessed. All the research and hours spent huddled over a computer screen were for nothing. He was pushing forty and very much alone. His last relationship had ended nearly five years ago and his social life had waned to the occasional dinner with acquaintances. He'd dedicated his life to a madman and he had nothing to show for it aside from a sizeable advance and a house that was much too big for one man.

"But you're not alone," the voice said. "You'll never be alone again. You have me, Charles. And I have such plans for you. Charles and Tucker. Tucker and Charles. It has a wonderful ring to it, no?"

Charles didn't answer. His mind was elsewhere. He tried his best to focus on the task at hand. The chair was wobbly, the legs uneven. He'd meant to fix it but it hardly mattered now.

He stood up, one foot first testing the creaking wood, then the other. For a moment, he thought he'd lose his balance but the chair evened out.

He grabbed onto the rope, made certain it was tight enough. It felt rough and thick in his hands. He'd purchased it from a fishing supplies store. The man eyed him suspiciously when he checked out. It was the only item in his basket.

The voice laughed. "Do you really think hanging yourself is a good idea? I mean, how do you know what's on the other side? How do you know it won't be me waiting for you?"

"Shut up." It was the first time he'd spoken in the last day. His voice was raspy and he sounded like a scared child.

"I'm not sure how many more times I have to say this. Let me spell it out for you as simply as possible. I. Am. In. Charge. Where you go, I go. Suicide is not a permanent solution because your problem is not temporary. You are me. You're Tucker Ashton."

He shook his head. "No, I'm not. I'm nothing like you."

"You're a terrible liar."

"I'll never be like you."

"Keep telling yourself that."

Tears tickled his cheeks. He didn't want to die. That was the worst part about it. He just wanted to leave this nightmare behind and live a somewhat normal life: marriage, kids, a steady job. It was a simple fantasy but he knew it wasn't an option anymore. He'd dug his own hole and he could no longer see the surface. There was only darkness down here. Pure, suffocating darkness.

"That's an analogy I can get behind. I think I've rubbed off on you."

Charles opened his mouth to respond but it was useless. He wasn't sure what he believed but he prayed he wouldn't see Tucker's horrid face when his neck snapped. He hoped he could close his eyes for good without hearing sobbing mothers and studying lifeless bodies. He hoped wherever he was going was better than this.

He tightened the noose around his neck, hung from the banister above, and kicked away the chair from beneath his feet.

In the moments before he finally died, when the lack of blood flow played tricks with his failing brain, he thought he saw the front door creak open as if from a breeze. He thought he saw a figure standing there: tall and impossibly skinny, a skeleton with just enough skin to qualify as a human.

No, not a human.

A monster.

TWO

IVY LONGWOOD DID not scream when she saw the blood. It was not the first time after all, nor would it be the last. She'd seen it once in reality several years back and now, over the last few months, it appeared nearly everywhere she went. Which made her day-to-day duties somewhat difficult.

Driving became impossible. She would see a wounded man, flesh gouged and bleeding into the street. Her hands would clutch the wheel and she'd swerve into oncoming traffic only to find, moments later, the man was a crossing guard or a postal worker, something much more benign than a victim of murder.

And then there was her job. She'd taught tenth grade English at a small, private school just north of Portland, Oregon. The kids were good, rowdy but much better than those at public school. A few weeks ago, while writing notes on the board for *Fiddler on the Roof*, she'd heard a sound behind her, something like sucking and biting.

She spun around, certain Tommy and Melinda were making out again. This would be their final warning. She would follow through with her threat of separating them. But the kids were busy writing

4

notes, Tommy and Melinda among them, neither set of lips locked with the other.

The sound came from behind the desks, near the back of the room, where a body lay on the floor. Most of its flesh had been torn way, exposing what lay beneath. She saw bone and muscle and organs. And blood, of course. Always so much blood.

Huddled over the body was a figure, its skin pale and ghostly. It went on eating for a few moments, chewing on something that looked like a spleen, before it sensed her watching. It dropped its meal and turned its head.

And smiled before it stood up and pounced toward her.

Moments later, the principal stood in the doorway, her face contorted with worry and revulsion.

Ivy hadn't realized she was screaming.

In the back of the classroom the body and the figure were gone. And by the end of the school day, she was kindly asked to take an extended leave of absence. Which later became permanent.

Now, as Ivy's sister Mariah paced her kitchen and spoke much too fast, Ivy once again tried to ignore the blood. It covered the floor, red puddles seeping into the hardwood. There were footprints all along it. Mariah's shoes were ruined with dark stains, though she didn't seem to notice.

Of course she doesn't notice. Because it's not real. None of this is real.

"Are you even listening?" Mariah said.

Ivy shook her head and sipped her coffee, pretending to enjoy the bitterness. Her sister brewed it strong and thick like mud. No amount of cream and sugar could make it drinkable. "Of course I'm listening."

"Then tell me what I just said. Any of it." Mariah looked much like their mother in that moment and, Ivy supposed, had been forced to play the part as of late. She had no children yet but she treated Ivy like one. And with good reason.

"Probably something about how my behavior is what you'd call unhealthy and that even though my therapist isn't helping I should try another one. And another. Until I find one that can cure me. Oh, and you must have mentioned Marlowe, right?"

Mariah sighed and began to wash the dishes. It was her way of keeping her shit together. The water came out red. "Something along those lines. I wish you'd listen to me more. I'm your sister. I'm your *family.*"

"I know," Ivy said. "I'm sorry." It was the truth, though she would not change her mind about getting on that plane tomorrow morning.

"Why now?" Mariah said, scrubbing at some phantom stain on her silverware. "Why, years later, do you feel the need to go to that ... cesspool?"

"I've heard it's nice this time of year."

"Be serious for a minute, will you?"

It was Ivy's turn to sigh. "What do you want me to say? I don't *know* why. It's just something I need to do. I bet if I told my shrink, he'd approve of the trip."

"If you told your shrink," Mariah said, "he'd probably cuff you to the chair and send you to someplace with padded rooms."

Ivy smiled. There was nothing funny about the joke, at least not on the surface, but she was exhausted. She laughed. Mariah followed.

"You really don't think this is a bad idea?" Mariah said. She lifted a glass and dried it with a rag.

Ivy shrugged. "What's the worst that could happen? It's pretty much a ghost town. There's hardly anybody living there. I'll walk around, face some demons, and come back with a clear head. I promise."

"Cross your heart?"

"And hope to die." She winced at the last part.

"Why didn't you go earlier?" Mariah said. She finally finished cleaning and sat down across the table. "You know, when Scott ..." She didn't finish the sentence. There was always an ellipsis when she mentioned Scott's name.

Ivy shook her head. "I don't know. I just didn't feel the need until recently."

Until you started seeing dead people and monsters, you mean.

In the corner of the kitchen, one of the cabinets had been left open. Flies buzzed in delight above the severed fingers that sat next to a jar of peanut butter.

"You see it right now, don't you?" Mariah followed her line of sight.

"See what?"

"The blood."

"No," Ivy lied. "I'm just tired is all." Before her sister could ask any more questions, she stood, drained her coffee in the sink, and hugged Mariah. "It's just a trip to get some closure. There's nothing more to it than that."

"I hope so."

From the corner of her eye, she saw one of the severed fingers plop onto the floor.

The flies followed.

That night, she didn't bother trying to sleep. It had become a lost cause.

Ivy could hear her sister snoring through the paper-thin walls. It kept her up most nights, in addition to the dreams and the visions, but she had no room to complain. It wasn't her house. Mariah had been nice enough to let Ivy move in while she got her shit together. She'd only planned on staying for a few months at most.

That had been two years ago.

Right after Scott …

There it was again. That damned ellipsis. She wondered if she'd ever be able to say or think his name without the thought dragging into obscurity. She didn't want to forget him. That was impossible. But it would be nice to put a period at the end of his sentence.

She wiped a stray tear from her eyes. In all the time she'd spent with Mariah, Ivy had never cried in front of her. It was tough to wear such a mask. She saved her sobbing for the night, when the darkness hid her eyes. She covered her mouth to keep from making too much noise. The paper-thin walls worked both ways.

She turned over and positioned herself as if spooning, though the other side of the bed was empty. She touched the sheet. It was frigid, always so damned cold.

That's because no one sleeps there anymore.

It was the same bed from her apartment with Scott. Much of the other furniture now lay in a storage unit. Even though the queen-sized mattress was much too big for the guest room, she'd insisted. Though she'd never admitted it to Mariah or even her therapist, the sheets had not been washed since the night Scott died. His side was still slightly indented, even after all this time. She didn't dare lie there, lest the slight dip vanish. Her side was yellowed with sweat and time and many tears. She knew it wasn't healthy to hold on like this. That's why she was going to Marlowe.

That and the fact she'd been called there.

That's what all this was: the blood, the death, the pale figure—all of it. Something was pulling her toward the town where Tucker Ashton had once lived. The place where he'd killed hundreds after his road trip from hell.

But before heading back to his hometown, he'd made one last stop just north of Portland, Oregon. Down the street from a small, private school where a young couple had met and fallen in love.

Ivy had been running late that night. She'd grabbed dinner and drinks with the girls, told Scott not to wait up.

The moment she walked through the door she knew something was wrong. She could feel it in the air, a sense of dread so thick it was palpable. The smell hit her next: warm, coppery blood. The same smell she sensed so often these days.

There were red footsteps, just like those in the kitchen earlier. She followed them, wondering if she ought to call the cops. If Scott was in trouble …

When she reached the bathroom she saw Scott was not just in trouble.

He was dead.

He lay in the bathtub, his clothes in a pile on the floor. They were badly torn, as though they'd been through a wood chipper. Scott looked similar. His skin had been shredded. Much of his insides were on the outside. His eyes were gone, two empty caverns in their place. On the wall, written in nearly perfect letters with her boyfriend's innards, was a simple phrase. The same phrase she'd been seeing in recent times.

The same phrase that had made her decide to book the plane and rental car.

I'll be seeing you.

Ivy hid another sob and pretended Scott was there to comfort her. She touched the cold sheets as if they were warm skin.

In the darkness she heard a dripping sound.

It was not a leaky faucet.

"There's still time to think this through," Mariah said. She parked in the drop-off lane, her wheel kicking the curb. The car shook before evening out.

"Believe me, I've had plenty of time to think it through." Ivy reached a hand across the passenger seat and fixed a loosed strand of her sister's hair.

"Can I ask you a question?" Mariah said.

"Fine but it's got to be one you haven't already asked a million times." Ivy studied the clock. She had another hour before her flight. Earlier, she'd been on the lookout for a traffic jam or a car crash, some sort of cosmic sign. Perhaps she wasn't meant to go to Marlowe after all. But the road had been clear, more like a holiday than Tuesday morning rush hour. How was that for a sign?

"What do you expect to find in that town?" Mariah's eyes were dark and tired.

"That, honey, is a good question. And when I come back with my shit together, I'll have an answer for you." She kissed her sister on the forehead, grabbed her bag from the back, and sped away before Mariah could convince her to stay behind.

She waved once on her way into the airport, trying to ignore the filthy windshield. Blood caked the glass, making it difficult for Ivy to see her sister's face.

After going through security, she was certain her flight would be delayed or canceled. Another wish for a sign that this was a bad idea, just like Mariah had been telling her. The screens told her the flight was on schedule. They were due in Logan airport ten minutes earlier than expected. The winds were on their side.

Ivy bought a coffee, this one much more drinkable than her sister's brew, and stepped into the bookstore kiosk. She doubted she could keep her mind steady enough to read but it was a long flight.

She fingered through romances and mysteries but one book in particular caught her eye. It was in the new releases section, nestled between an espionage thriller and a western.

The cover was simple enough: a close-up of a man's face. His eyes were vacant and his lips thin. The skin along his face was taut, the chin and cheek bones threatening to burst through. It wasn't hard to imagine the skull that lay beneath. She'd seen the face before, both in reality and nightmares.

She picked the book up and brought it to the register, gritting her teeth. She wasn't sure if she was scared or angry or both.

The girl behind the counter, hair dyed bleach blond and dimples pierced, eyed the cover. "This is our biggest seller this week. Why would you want to read something like that on a plane? Or anywhere for that matter? No offense."

Ivy shrugged and paid without answering.

The girl placed the book into a semi-transparent bag. Tucker Ashton's hellish face peeked through. The book's title was apt.

Birth of a Monster by Charles Williamson.

She thanked the girl and made her way to the terminal where the monitors and seats were soaked with red streaks. She chose to stand.

THREE

"YOU READY OR what?" Amy called from the living room.

"Just a minute," Zeke Evans said. "I've got to update the site and then we're good." It was a lie. He'd updated the site earlier that morning in bed, while Amy snored beside him. She always looked beautiful when she slept. In fact, sometimes Zeke would watch her for hours. There was something about the way her eyes were plastered shut, as if closed forever, that turned him on.

He checked his watch. They'd planned on leaving at nine to miss rush hour. The drive from Virginia to Massachusetts was roughly ten hours. That gave him five more minutes to admire his collection. The room was the second largest in their home. It served as his office, study, and man cave. It was not decorated with sports banners or swimsuit posters. The walls were covered with a different kind of memorabilia.

He'd been interviewed by several authors and journalists and even a documentary film crew. They always painted him as a weirdo. Intelligent, sure. A damned good journalist himself, sure. But no one in their right mind collected serial killer trinkets.

He begged to differ.

The collection was organized by killer. From left to right were sections for Ed Gein, Albert Fish, Ted Bundy, John Wayne Gacy, and of course, his all-time favorite, Tucker Ashton. He had more artifacts from Tucker than any other killer: pieces of clothing from his victims, rare taped interviews, childhood toys that had belonged to him, and—Zeke's most beloved items—Tucker's letters from prison.

These he kept in a binder, the pages protected within plastic sleeves. Though he'd scanned each one onto his computer, the originals still looked pristine. Most of the correspondence could be found on Zeke's site, killwithathrill.com, but many he kept private because of the subject matter. He'd never expected a reply back when, a year prior, he'd had a little too much to drink, scribbled a fan letter, and sent it to the asylum where his favorite killer had resided. Tucker had taken a liking to Zeke, respected his line of work, and kept in close contact from his cell up until the day he disappeared. Though that wasn't the right term.

That implied Tucker wasn't coming back.

Zeke opened his binder and flipped to the last page. The most recent letter was dated from two weeks ago. At first he'd thought it was a fake but the handwriting was spot on. He'd compared it to the other pages and there was no denying it.

Tucker was alive and well and he had plans for Zeke.

I hope this letter finds you well and I hope you've kept up the site. What you're doing is important work. Invaluable. I must ask a favor of you. Keep this one off of the web. It's for your eyes only. I'm coming back, Zeke. And I want you to be there when it happens. You can have the exclusive interview. Would you like that? You'd be a millionaire overnight. All you need to do is come to my home. That's where I'll be. In Marlowe. See you soon.

Tucker

Zeke had committed the words to memory. He read without blinking, a cartoonish smile on his face. This was the real deal. He was going to meet his hero, the man who made the rest of the greats look like jokes.

There was a knock at the door. "Car's all packed," Amy said.

He quickly closed the binder. She knew of the letters but not the most recent one. She thought they were just taking a road trip to visit the site of the Marlowe Massacre. To her it was a vacation instead of a pilgrimage. Tucker had asked for secrecy and Zeke intended to obey.

"Come in." He placed his laptop into its carrying case, tried to act casual. "I guess we'd better get going then."

Amy smiled. "I can't believe we're actually doing it, you know? I mean, I never thought I'd see this place."

He embraced her, kissed her with an urgency that hadn't dwindled in the year they'd been dating. When they'd first met, her hair was a standard brunette. Now it was green and she had twice as many piercings. He was rubbing off on her, which was, he must admit, a bit of a turn on. She was studying criminal justice, wanted to be a lawyer. Zeke knew there was a joke in there somewhere but she was too intoxicating to think hard on it. "You sure we packed everything?"

She nodded. "I triple-checked."

"Then let's get going, shall we?" He took her hand and led her out of his sanctuary. Before turning off the light, he caught a glimpse of the binder, still resting on the desk.

He smiled again as he closed the door and locked it behind him.

They had a long drive ahead of them.

"Son of a bitch," Ivy said under her breath as she flipped the page.

This Charles Williamson, apparently an adjunct professor at Syracuse University, had written his book as if it were fiction. He'd sensationalized the thing so it read more like a second rate horror novel than true crime. It wasn't that he'd made facts up but rather the way in which he presented them. He went into excruciating detail of Tucker Ashton's past. His parents were horrid. His childhood was terrible. And so, Charles Williamson argued, the birth of a killer was inevitable.

She called bullshit. No matter how bad life got, no matter how many curve balls it threw, you were in control of your own actions. She hadn't lashed out or hurt anyone after Brad, though she'd certainly thought about it.

She studied the cover again and, despite her growing anger, she shivered.

Tucker's eyes were too wide, his pupils too detailed. She swore for a moment she could see her own reflection in his iris, as if it wasn't a book at all but a real, skeletal face, inches away from her own.

"You think they'll ever find him?"

Ivy nearly screamed. She'd forgotten about the man sitting next to her, the man who'd already tried several times to initiate conversation. Small talk wasn't her specialty and she wasn't feeling very conversational.

"He's probably dead somewhere," Ivy said, flipping over the book so the back cover faced upward, the blurb claiming Williamson had painted a most disturbing portrait of America's newest infamous serial killer.

"I don't know about that." The man smiled. His Coke bottle glasses magnified his eyes twice their real size. There was a piece of food stuck to his front tooth, perhaps spinach. "It seems too convenient, you know? The guy escaped a maximum security asylum. It's like a movie or something."

She rolled her eyes and looked out the window. "I'm sure it will be soon enough."

He laughed as if they'd shared a joke, old pals instead of strangers. "Only in the movie, they'll probably have him rise from the dead or something. You can't end with him disappearing. Where's the fun in that?"

She didn't answer, lest she invite more of his babbling. Eventually, he took the hint.

Her neck was stiff and her body tense. She allowed herself to relax a bit, yawning and stretching. Her eyes grew heavy.

A few moments later she felt a tap on her shoulder. "I've got it," the man said, only his voice seemed deeper now. Perhaps her ears had popped again.

"Got what?" she said without looking.

"I know where he went. It's obvious, isn't it? He's gone to Marlowe. Why, yes, that's it. I'm positive. Never been more certain of anything in my pathetic little life. He's gone to Marlowe and he wants you to meet him there. That's where you're heading, isn't it? He'll show you where he's been and if you're lucky he might even bring you *with* him. And here's the best part: he'll kill again. Yes, ma'am, you can bet your money on it. He'll kill again and he'll never stop until the oceans are red and the blood drowns us all." The man began to giggle, a slow laugh at first, turning to a full-on howl.

She looked at him and wished she hadn't. He wasn't the same annoying man he'd been moments before. There was something wrong with him. He'd grown bloated and pale and there was a gaping hole where his throat should've been. It leaked red onto her seat, onto her arms. She tried to wipe it away but it was instantly replaced.

"What did I tell you?" the man said. Most of his teeth were gone. "We're all going to drown."

The blood gushed onto the floor, climbing until her ankles were covered, then her shins and knees, before rising to submerge her lower body. She made to scream but found she had no voice.

She struggled to stand but her seatbelt was stuck in place. No, not belt—*belts*. There were more than one, too many belts to count, each with their own clasps, holding her back. Trapping her. She tried to undo them but the metal was scalding. Her fingers grew red, the flesh blistering instantly.

"Just remember," the laughing man said. "He's chosen you for a reason. I'm not sure what it is, but you must be special." He reached into his mouth and, as casually as someone picking spinach from their teeth, ripped his jaw off, letting the blood flow even faster.

The plane flooded. It nosedived and began its descent toward the earth. All around there were screams and pleas and Ivy realized she was going to die just as she opened her eyes and saw daylight blinding her through the window.

The overhead speaker came alive. "Welcome to Boston, ladies and gentlemen. Thanks so much for flying with us today. Enjoy your stay."

"That was some flight, huh?" the man beside her said. He was no longer bloated and his throat was intact. "Haven't seen that much turbulence in a long time. It's like the plane wanted to turn itself around."

She nodded, held her neck, and tried to push back the panic attack.

There was only one seat belt across her waist. She undid it and tossed the buckles aside as if they had teeth.

FOUR

"ARE YOU FEELING okay?" Amy said. She'd been watching Zeke in her periphery for the last hour.

"You kidding? I'm great. Fantastic. Now that you mention it, though, I do have to take a piss. You mind if we pull over?" He nodded to a rest stop coming up on their right.

"Fine by me," Amy said, faking a smile. "You sure you're all right?"

He shrugged. "Maybe a little tired. I was up late working on the site. Not to mention I was excited about the trip. Like a kid on Christmas Eve."

She nodded and tried to hide her worry. "Yeah, I can't wait to get there."

"Do I look sick or something?" He pulled into the rest stop parking lot and looked at her for the first time in the last hour. For some odd reason, she thought he could read her mind. And if that were the case, he wouldn't like what he found.

She shook her head too quickly. "You look great, babe. Just making sure you're okay driving is all. Want me to take a turn?"

He parked and cut the engine, rubbed her leg. "I'm good for

now. Maybe at the next stop. You want a coffee?"

"Not yet." She took in her surroundings. There was a diner, its windows smeared with yellow stains, like they hadn't been washed since the place opened its doors. Across the way was a row of public bathrooms that looked ready to crumble from rust. She wondered how many truck drivers picked up hookers here, how many drugs had been purchased. She thought she saw a needle near the car.

"Suit yourself. Be back in a few minutes." He made to get out but paused. "Oh and, Amy?"

"Yeah?" *Don't read my mind. Don't read my mind.*

"I'm really glad you came. It means the world. I wouldn't want to go to Marlowe with anyone else. It's weird but the closer we get, it's like we're going home, you know? Like we've lived there all along."

"I wouldn't miss it for the world. Hurry back. It'll be rush hour before you know it. You know how cranky you get in traffic."

She watched him go. His walk had changed. When they'd first met, he stepped with an air of confidence. Not so much that he was into himself. He just seemed to know who he was and what he liked, which had initially drew Amy to him. Now, though, he moved slowly, his arms hanging like he was sleepwalking.

Which was a very real possibility. She often woke in the middle of the night to an empty bed. She'd find him in his office, huddled over his desk and whispering something to himself, the words usually too soft to make out. The office door would be open, the keys dangling out of the lock. That's how she'd known he was sleeping. Zeke guarded his study like it was a treasury. It wasn't that he didn't trust her, he insisted, he was just neurotic about his collection. Nothing more to it than that.

A couple weeks ago, he'd woken her as he shuffled out of the bedroom and down the hall. She'd followed, keeping her steps quiet. Didn't they say you weren't supposed to wake a sleepwalker? He unlocked the door and sat at his desk. He mumbled something, his voice changing tone every so often as if he were speaking *with* someone. He tore a piece of paper from a notebook. He read aloud as he wrote: something about Tucker Ashton calling Zeke to Marlowe for his big return. Like the guy was writing from the grave or something. Everyone knew he was dead. The world's most popular killer didn't just up and disappear. If he was alive, surely he would've killed again by now. For the most part, serial murderers wanted to get caught. But Zeke refused to accept this. Zeke believed he was out there somewhere.

When they'd started seeing each other, she thought the serial killer thing was an odd but harmless hobby, something he'd managed to turn into a business. But with Tucker it was different, more of an obsession. A compulsion.

The bathroom doors opened. Zeke walked into the diner without looking back into the car. She was grateful. His sleepwalking wasn't the only strange thing about him lately. His eyes were ... different somehow. She couldn't explain it. It was as if they'd been plucked from another source and placed into his skull. It got under her skin in a way she couldn't vocalize. Combine that with his growing obsession with finding Tucker and you had the ever-expanding feeling of dread in her gut.

And Amy had always trusted her gut. When she'd received a call in the middle of the night two years ago, she'd known her mother had died. She didn't know the details, that a drunk driver had dropped his cigarette into his crotch and swerved onto the sidewalk. But she'd been certain her mother wouldn't be visiting any time soon. Now, just like that night, she had a hunch this trip was a bad idea. Whatever awaited them in Marlowe wasn't *worth* the wait.

She tried to push the thoughts aside, told herself she was being silly.

Zeke paid the waitress at the bar and grabbed a large cup of coffee. As he turned toward the front door, she fought the urge to drive off.

Those eyes, she thought. *They're not his. They belong to someone else.*

He walked—shambled—toward the car. He did not smile when he caught her looking.

There's something seriously wrong here. It's not just bad vibes.

A few feet from the door, sipping his coffee. Staring with his stranger's eyes.

If you're going to leave, now's the time. The last *time. Because any later will be too late.*

She frowned. What the hell did that mean?

Zeke reached the car and opened the door. "Sorry I took so long. I think the waitress was on something and the line was out the door."

She smiled. "How's the coffee?"

"Fine, I guess. Try a sip."

She lifted the cup. It was bitter to the point of no return, tasted more like motor oil. Zeke apparently hadn't noticed.

"You ready?" He strapped on his seatbelt.

She opened her mouth to respond but he was already driving. The dirty diner and rusty bathrooms shrank in the rearview as their car merged back onto I-95. She turned on the radio and tried to forget her last train of thought but it was useless.

Any later will be too late.

"You won't believe the rental car they gave me," Ivy said into the phone in between drags of her cigarette. She spoke like nothing was wrong, like she was off on some tropical vacation. Blowing off steam instead of fighting off demons.

"A Jaguar?" Mariah's voice seemed even farther away than the thousand miles that separated them.

"Even better."

"A Ferrari."

"It's a PT Cruiser." She looked at her vehicle, the sole car in the parking lot of the convenience store. According to her GPS, it was the last stop before Marlowe.

"Who did you have to blow for that?"

Ivy knew it was a joke but she winced. She hadn't been with anyone since Scott. To be honest, she hadn't had the urge to speak to another man, let alone sleep with one. Her libido had all but vanished, along with her sanity.

"Ivy, you still there?"

She shook her head. "Yeah, sorry. I'm here."

"You're smoking again, aren't you?"

She tossed the cigarette onto the ground, putting it out with her foot. "I don't know what you're talking about."

"Just because you're on the phone and not in front of my face doesn't mean I can't smell bullshit. You've always been a terrible liar."

"I'm as honest as they come."

"If you're so honest, then tell me what you see right now? Not the convenience store or the gas pumps. The other stuff. Tell me about the blood."

Ivy froze. She'd never opened up about the carnage she saw on a daily basis. She'd simply told Mariah there was a bit of blood. In reality—using the term loosely—it varied. Sometimes, there was only a smear along a wall. Then there were the bad days, the days when you couldn't block out the death to save your life.

Today was a bad day.

Liquid spilled into the nearby sewer grate but it hadn't rained recently. The blood seemed to originate from the store, leaking from underneath the front doors. On either side of the road, for as far as you could see, were trees. And on many of those trees hung heads, the eyes open as if watching, the mouths frozen as if screaming.

"You know," Ivy said, "you'd think it would be bad out here, considering how close I am to Marlowe, but I've got to say it's the opposite. I haven't seen anything since we landed."

Mariah sighed, the sound harsh in Ivy's ear. "Cut the shit."

"I'm telling the truth. I think this place, this trip, really is helping. Which is exactly what I've been saying all along. You can stop worrying, okay? I'm in good shape." She looked at the sign for Marlowe down the road. Someone had spray-painted over the words. She couldn't make out the message but she had a feeling it wasn't welcoming.

"Promise me one thing," Mariah said.

"You know I'm bad at promises."

"Promise you'll get the hell out of there if something goes wrong."

Ivy's heart stopped for a moment. "Wrong? Like what?"

"Just promise."

"I pinkie swear and hope to die."

"That's not how it goes." Mariah said something else but her voice cut out.

"Sis, you there?" Her words were lost in a fit of static. "The reception's awful out here. Listen, I'll call you later, okay? Love you."

She listened to the distortion for a moment longer before hanging up.

Her stomach grumbled. She hadn't eaten since this morning, when she'd forced down a stale coffee roll back home. She stepped around the stream of blood and went inside the store.

A large man sat behind the counter, his gut threatening to burst through his stained shirt. He chewed something she at first thought was tobacco but then he blew a pink bubble that popped onto his lips.

His cheeks reddened as he caught her staring. He sucked the

wad back into his mouth and nodded. "Afternoon. Need any help?"

"Point me in the direction of your coffee and junk food and I'll be on my way."

"Last aisle on the left." He pretended to read a crumpled newspaper while she looked through the food but every so often she caught him staring at her ass. He seemed harmless enough but out here, this close to Tucker Ashton's hometown, she didn't quite trust anyone. It was irrational, she knew. The people had nothing to do with the murders but she couldn't shake the feeling.

She settled on her snacks—beef jerky, no-name brand potato chips, and a bag of circus peanuts for good measure—and sifted through the coffee flavors. The bells above the front door jingled as two customers—a man and a woman—stepped inside. The man was talking too quickly, barely breathing between words, and the girl eyed him with concern.

"More coffee," the guy said. "Then I'll be fine."

"I think you've had more than enough," the girl said. "And I told you I'd drive. You look exhausted. Why don't you take a nap and let me drive the rest of the way?"

The guy reached Ivy's aisle. "Are you kidding? Look at how close we are. I want to be awake for all of this. Hell, I don't want to blink if I can help it."

For some odd reason, Ivy didn't want to look at the man's eyes, let alone talk to him. It was the same sensation she'd had back on the plane, only her neighbor hadn't been quite as ... what was the word?

Menacing.

She frowned, not sure why she'd settled on such a term, but it seemed fitting. On the surface, the guy seemed normal enough: late twenties or early thirties, black hair, a five o'clock shadow bordering on nightfall, but his eyes—his eyes were what made Ivy's stomach drop not unlike the rough descent from her nightmare.

She wasn't sure *how* she knew but she was certain of one thing.

The man's eyes were not good. Worse yet, she could've sworn she'd seen them before, though she couldn't pinpoint where. She forced herself to look away, pay him no mind, and blindly pour the nearest pot of coffee into her cup. She tossed in sugar and milk and hurried before the man reached the snacks.

In the reflection of the nearest freezer door, Ivy noticed the girl staring. Her eyes were much saner. Much more innocent. She seemed helpless, like she'd been kidnapped and was trying to signal Ivy's help. Surely that wasn't the case. Surely Ivy was overtired, her imagination overactive.

The longer Ivy stared at the reflection, the more obscure it grew. Not because her eyes went out of focus but because blood began to seep from an unseen crack near the ice cream. It covered all the frozen items until even the highest shelf, filled with yogurt, was submerged. The glass looked ready to crack from the pressure and she once again had the sensation of impending doom, like if the blood was released, she would drown within moments.

It was the worst vision she'd had yet. The other freezers followed suit until every unit was filled with dark red. She held onto the nearest rack for support and noticed the magazines were sodden, their pages stuck together. They smelled of mold and copper. Her pulse raced and she grew dizzy.

It's that guy and his weird eyes. He's bad news and you need to get the hell out of here.

She wasn't sure what to make of the premonition but she also wasn't about to question it. She sped to the counter, threw down a ten-dollar bill, and told the bubble gum attendant to keep the change.

On her way out she heard the guy spewing facts about Marlowe but more specifically about its most famous resident. He sounded like he was giving a lecture on his most beloved subject, only instead of nerding out over physics, he spoke of victims and torture.

Ivy forced back her vertigo as she stepped into the PT Cruiser—looking very much like a hearse now—and sped out of the parking lot. In the rearview mirror, the blood still flowed from the store. It seemed to follow her, willing her forward on her journey.

The sign with the graffiti appeared on her left but she was going too fast to read its message.

Something told her that was for the best.

FIVE

ON THE OTHER side of Marlowe, riding along the same road, a man named Ethan Roberts slammed his fist against the steering wheel and uttered several creative curse words. He stepped on the gas pedal of his car, a 2002 Honda Civic that had been on its last legs for the past three years, but it wouldn't go any faster. His speedometer read one hundred, but it felt like he was barely pushing thirty.

He needn't look in his rearview to see the police cruisers. There were two of them now, gaining quickly. Their lights spilled red and blue onto the road before him, making him feel like he was at a carnival. His eyes played tricks. In the trees on either side he swore he saw shapes, humanoid shapes that watched and waited and used the shadows to their advantage. He could've blamed this on his nerves or the high-speed chase but there was more to it than that.

In the back seat was a garbage bag filled with various prescription pills. Mostly pain killers. Medicines for people who were in pain but also those who were addicted. It was the latter group that would make Ethan money but it was the former group that made him agree to the robbery in the first place.

His brother Andrew had been selling for years now, in and out of prison since high school. Fresh off a five-year sentence, he swore off all illegal activity. Until two weeks ago when he'd met Ethan at the Ipswich Sports Bar. They didn't speak much anymore. Andrew only called when he needed something. The last time they'd spent any time together had been the ride home from prison.

He could see it in Andrew's face that night, hear it in his salesman-like voice. He may have been a criminal but he was quite persuasive. Charming even. "I've got something planned," he'd said. "Something big. And I need your help."

"No way," Ethan said like a reflex. "Whatever it is, count me out. Don't even tell me about it. In fact, I'm walking away now." Andrew grabbed his arm. No one took notice. The music was loud and the clientele was louder.

"Hear me out, okay? There's money at stake. A lot of it if we play our cards right. And if we're being honest, buddy, you need money these days."

Ethan gritted his teeth and pulled his arm away.

"You want to hit me, don't you?" Andrew said. "I know that look. I've been on the other end of it most of my life. I get it. But I'm strapped for cash and you're drowning in medical bills. I've heard chemo is expensive."

Instead of hitting him, Ethan went slack. His eyes clouded and he pretended he had to piss.

"I'll be here when you get back," Andrew said. "Then we can talk. Things are going to work out with this one. Your girl's gonna have all the treatments she needs." That smug grin of his again, like he was convincing Ethan to sign up for a magazine subscription instead of robbing a pharmacy.

The bathroom was a single toilet that was usually clogged and a sink that never seemed to have hot water. The mirror was busted into three sections. He wondered who had hated their reflection enough to smash it. At that moment, Ethan hadn't blamed them.

Though he'd said no to Andrew, he'd already changed his mind on the walk across the bar. It wasn't because he was easily persuaded. It was because Andrew had been right about one thing. Chemo *was* expensive. His daughter, Lisa, who preferred to go by *Princess* Lisa, had been diagnosed the prior year. Leukemia. Luckily, it was in the early stages and highly treatable. She was taking the treatments like a champ, drew and colored while she was hooked up to poison.

But the prices were astronomical. He'd thought his insurance was good until the bills started coming. He worked as a loan officer at the Ipswich Cooperative Bank and he'd picked up several night shifts at the local gas station. It still wasn't enough.

Alexis worked too but his wife's schedule had to be flexible. She was the one that took their girl to the appointments, of which there were plenty.

"You're stupid if you agree to this," Ethan said to his reflection. "Whatever scheme he has, you should just walk away." But he knew he wouldn't. He knew he'd already been reeled in.

A few minutes later he sat back down at the table. Andrew was still smiling, as if he hadn't moved an inch since Ethan left. On the table were two fresh beers. Ethan drained his within seconds. He belched. "Say what you've got to say and make it quick."

"It'll take no more than ten minutes. You'll be in and out and debt free."

The worst part, the part that made Ethan scream those creative curses now, was he'd actually believed Andrew.

Up ahead there was only darkness, like he could drive forever and never reach his destination. But in a few miles, he'd pass the Marlowe town line. Then he'd lose the cops. He knew his way around, had grown up there, though he hadn't been back in years, not since just before the massacre. Supposedly, more than half the town up and left. He would've done the same had he still been living there.

Tucker Ashton was bad news, except that wasn't a strong enough term. It may have sounded cheesy but the guy was pure evil. Had been since they were children. Ethan had promised himself never to go back to Marlowe but the drop off was there. The second he got the money he'd speed back out even faster, cops be damned.

The closer he got, the more his periphery swam with movement. Those shapes were everywhere now. He didn't dare take his eye off the road. Not because he worried he'd lose control. He'd lost that miles back when he busted through the back door of a pharmacy and bagged every pill on the list Andrew had written. No, it was much simpler than that.

He knew whatever he'd see in the trees would make him scream.

He passed the welcome sign and felt something wash over him. A feeling in the air, something stirring with electricity like the world's worst thunderstorm was on its way.

Or worse.

"Pull over," Zeke said.

"Already? We just got back on the road." There was a hint of annoyance in Amy's voice but she hid it well. Their relationship was still in its infancy. They rarely argued, rarely showed anything but utter affection, but he could tell Amy was less than pleased.

"I'll be quick."

"You should've just gone in the store." She used her turn signal, as if they weren't alone on the road, and pulled over to the curb.

"I don't have to piss. And this is the wrong side."

"What do you mean?"

Without answering, he grabbed his camera from the backseat, opened the passenger side door, and jogged across the street. Despite Amy's insistence that she man the wheel for a while, he wasn't the least bit tired. Quite the opposite. He felt alive in a way he hadn't in years. The closest sensation he could think of was the thrill he got reading Tucker's letters, especially the most recent, but this—this took the fucking cake.

He stopped in front of the green road sign, the one that welcomed them to Marlowe, Massachusetts, population of ten thousand, though it was much less these days. Someone had spray painted the text. The artist had drawn horns coming out of the town's name, like the word was a face just waiting to open its eyes. How cute.

That wasn't the best part, though. They'd also scribbled out two words and managed to change the sign's meaning. It was perfect in a way he couldn't even begin to describe. He raised the camera and peered through the screen.

He hadn't been joking earlier. He felt as if they were heading *for* home instead of away from it.

Which made the deletion all the more fitting.

"You coming?" Amy called from across the way. She fidgeted in her seat. She did not seem as excited. He hoped her interest didn't continue to wane. He needed her alert and happy, needed her to share in his elation when he came face to face with his hero. Perhaps he'd tell her as much tonight.

But Tucker told you to keep it a secret.

Then there was the issue of finding him. Where would Ashton

be? How would Zeke know where to look? Something told him he'd figure it out as he went. This was much more than a vacation or business trip. It had all the markings of a game changer. The interview could make him millions, sure, but that was the proverbial icing on the cake. The money was great but the feeling in the air, the sensation of his skin coming alive with a pleasant tingling, told him he was on the path to something special.

"Be right there." He snapped several photos, the last of which zoomed in on the painted-over words. He smiled as he read them aloud. The artist had removed "before highway" so that it simply read—

"Last stop."

He jogged back to the car and told Amy to step on it.

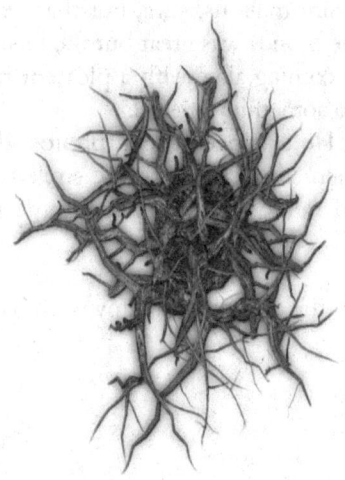

The following excerpts were taken from Charles Williamson's *Birth of a Monster*, published on the day of his death.

In a strange sort of way, Tucker Ashton's birth was a miracle.

His parents had been plagued with two miscarriages and one stillborn. They were convinced a child was out of the picture. In fact, they'd all but stopped trying by the time Diana Ashton—formerly Diana Stewart—conceived for the fourth and final time. She surprised her husband during his thirty-sixth birthday party. Surrounded by friends, mostly hers, and family members, also mostly hers, Brad Ashton closed his eyes while the cake was presented on the table before him. It did not say "Happy Birthday" as he'd been led to believe. Instead three other words were printed in blue frosting, the lettering quite amateurish according to accounts.

It's a boy.

Brad Ashton had never wanted a child to begin with and later, after his only son was born, he would often remind the boy of this. On those sleepless nights of early parenthood, of which there were plenty due to Tucker's colic, Brad would whisper how he would've been much better off without his boy. Diana would hear Brad repeating the words over and over, like a personal mantra, and choose to ignore them. She blamed his behavior on the stress of being a new father. Though at a certain point, she was forced to see the truth: her husband had issues that he'd kept from her. And for good reason.

It comes as no surprise that Tucker developed social issues by the time he reached high school. A quiet child, he secretly craved the attention he did not receive at home. His mother worked nights at the local grocery store, which left Tucker alone with his father after a long day's shift at one of Marlowe's many mills. There was rarely any interaction between the two when Diana was absent. Brad would offer his son a plate of fish sticks or pizza rolls and retire to his chair in the living room to watch his television programs: usually police procedurals but he settled for the occasional court room drama.

Though not one for technology (Brad Ashton often insisted he was born in the wrong time), Diana convinced him to buy Tucker his own computer.

"Why the hell would we do that?" Brad posed. "The kid's just going to get himself into trouble. That or he'll download enough porn to fry the thing with a virus."

"Don't be ridiculous," Diana said. "He can use it for homework and keep in touch with his friends."

Brad laughed, took a sip of beer (always PBR—not because of the cheap price tag but because he genuinely enjoyed the taste), and reminded her Tucker did not have any friends.

Brad was right about two things.

Firstly, Tucker did not have any companions to speak of. He spent time with boys from school, played the occasional round of ultimate Frisbee, but he hadn't grown close to anyone. His interpersonal skills were nearly nonexistent.

Secondly, that first family computer, placed in the finished basement in which Tucker spent so much time (and which would later become a prison of sorts) proved lucrative in his descent into madness.

Tucker did indeed get himself into trouble.

From the start, Tucker took to the computer like most boys his age (thirteen, going on fourteen) took to skateboarding or sneaking into R-rated movies. He quickly grew bored with the Internet. Sure, there was porn and access to as many horror films as one could imagine but neither held his interest. He begged his parents to buy him a webcam. For his friends, he suggested. He'd been growing close with a couple boys in his class. And a girl too. Just like they'd asked. Most of his classmates later denied any relationship, though at the time, Diana was inclined to believe her son was finally shedding his shyness.

He eventually convinced his parents and for his fourteenth birthday was presented with a camera that cost more than the family's annual vacation to Bar Harbor, so said Brad. In truth, the model was much less than the computer itself.

Tucker used his new camera for two things.

The first, taking random videos and posting them to YouTube, Daily Motion, and any other video sharing sites he could find, spoke volumes toward his need for affection but more so his need to be noticed. This would later inform the way in which he killed.

The second, filming strangers as they walked by the house and watching the videos repeatedly, is what psychologists refer to as "distancing." Tucker filmed these individuals so they weren't real. Once they graced the computer screen, they were simply objects. There grew a disconnect between the way in which Tucker viewed the world through a screen and the actual world he lived in.

This combination would later birth, so to speak, Tucker's calling card. It wasn't worth the killing if no one noticed, which is why he chose to film his victims and post the videos online.

Then he would be noticed.

Diana Ashton was killed roughly one year after her son began uploading videos. He had started with small animals. Several videos of cats, dogs, and squirrels were recovered, though many more are thought to be lost. Diana traveled to the city for a coworker's wedding which she couldn't convince Brad to attend. She was running late, was forced to park in a garage several blocks from the venue. A man who was later gunned down by police stepped from behind a neighboring SUV and cracked Diana's skull with a hammer. Officials assured Brad and Tucker she died quickly and without pain.

The assailant's name was Devon Sanfilippo. His toxicology report showed excessive alcohol and methamphetamines the night he mugged Diana. He screamed at police, charged the two cruisers that cornered him near Boston Common. The scene was played several times on the nightly news in the weeks after the incident.

Tucker watched it as often as he could. He saved it onto his computer's desktop.

With Diana gone, Brad did not bother to hide his alcoholic tendencies, something which family members had speculated and now confirmed. The PBR became less about taste and more about sheer numbers. Not satisfied drinking at home, especially with the son he'd never wanted, he took to the Marlowe Pub on most nights and became one of their most frequent customers.

Brad became increasingly suspicious that Tucker was "sick in the head." He took to locking his son in the basement, first while he was at the pub but then the routine spread to nights he spent home as well. Brad often forgot to let him out.

When the sole light bulb eventually burned out, Brad did not replace it. On nights he stole a glance through the keyhole, he saw only his son's face, faintly illuminated by the computer screen, his eyes unblinking, his face expressionless.

It was in the darkness of this finished basement, left alone for so very long, that Tucker Ashton the killer was born. Unlike his first birth, it would not prove to be a miracle.

SIX

As ETHAN ROBERTS passed through the town line, the cop cars vanished. There was no transition. One moment there were cascading lights blinding him in the rearview and the next there was only darkness. He told himself this was a trick of his eyes. He was exhausted, not just from tonight's burglary but from the past six months, from Lisa's diagnosis, from the toll it took on his marriage.

One mile into Marlowe, Ethan turned right on River Road, a stretch of privately owned land that ran parallel to the town river. As a kid, before his family moved away, he'd fished here, rounded first base with girls, even told a ghost story or two.

Now, as slowed the car to a stop and turned the front end toward the river, he wished he'd never recited such tales. In the darkness, he imagined things creeping among the shadows. It was the same sensation he'd experienced during the chase, like something was always one step away from revealing itself. His mind conjured skeletons and slimy appendages but they didn't do his fear justice.

He put the car into neutral. It was stolen from several towns over and dropped off at a department store parking lot, where Ethan picked it up. Andrew couldn't take part in the heist, he'd insisted. He was on parole, after all, and he didn't plan on ever going back to prison. Ethan was on his own. He grabbed the bag of pills and let his foot off the brake.

On the way out of the car, his wallet fell from his pocket and he forced back a yelp. He was not worried about money. There wasn't any cash within the cheap leather and most of his credit cards were maxed out. But behind those cards was a folded-up picture Lisa had drawn days before she'd been diagnosed.

Ethan dropped the pills, used his phone for light. The darkness out here, void of any street lamps, was complete. Even the moon seemed not to exist. He hyperventilated as he searched the ground, thinking the wallet was still in the car.

A moment after the vehicle crashed into the river, he felt the smooth rectangle. He used his phone for light, searched the contents until he found the piece of paper. It looked much older than six months. The corners were badly folded and there was a small tear that seemed to grow each time he viewed the picture.

Ought to get it laminated if I make it out of here.

He froze and frowned.

If? Why had his mind chosen such a word? Surely he meant *when*. Surely his nerves were getting the best of him.

He unfolded the picture and held the phone close. Lisa had drawn herself as a princess, hence her nickname. The stick figure version of his daughter stood on the peak of a castle, overseeing a kingdom that stretched for miles. She held a sword, bedazzled with jewels, but a sword nonetheless. In the distance a dragon approached. Before, it had looked like a googly-eyed frog but now there was something sinister about the beast. Were its eyes larger? Redder?

"You look like a superhero," Ethan had said when Lisa handed him the picture.

She'd nodded, proud. "Dragons don't scare me. I'm brave."

"You certainly are," he'd said. Now he said it again to himself.

He held the picture away for fear of spilling a tear onto the page. It was already deteriorating too quickly. He couldn't afford any more damage. He folded it back up and walked along the road. Without a car, the trip would take roughly forty-five minutes, thirty if he pushed it. But the pills were heavy and his exhaustion was cutting through the adrenaline.

That and he still wasn't keen on heading deeper into town.

He walked for a few yards before stopping again. He looked into the sky and noticed the stars were gone. He could've blamed it on the weather, perhaps a passing storm, but he'd checked the weather forecast and there wasn't a projected cloud in sight. Out here, on this private road, he should've been able to see every constellation, make out the big dipper with ease. But there was nothing up there, only total blackness.

Even the stars are afraid of Tucker Ashton.

He waved the thought off. Tucker was dead. His escape was perhaps the mystery of the decade but he wasn't coming back to Marlowe. Even if he *was* alive, why come home?

To finish what he started. To kill the rest of them.

He didn't like the way his thoughts were headed. He hung the bag over his shoulder and started walking again, albeit much faster this time. The drop-off was in the heart of town, at Hotel Marlowe, and he wanted to get this over with.

He did his best not to look at the sky, lest he be reminded of the anomaly.

Not to mention the things in his periphery.

A drink was in order.

Ivy parked in front of the pub across from Hotel Marlowe. Downtown was a line of shops that seemed very much out of place and time. There was a drug store that advertised cough syrup and malt shakes. There was a theater with sun-faded posters in the window, the films decades old. The shoe cobbler, sitting between a consignment shop and bookstore, looked ready to topple over. Surely it saw no business, yet it was there, in front of her, with the hours proudly displayed on the entrance.

Even the hotel looked ancient. There was a marquee out front, with lights that had dimmed with time. She imagined the place swimming with activity during the roaring twenties, girls with bobbed hair holding the arms of men with pressed suits, stepping out of cars that looked like her rental.

Ivy got the sense she'd passed through more than just a town line back there, whatever that meant.

Her sister's voice echoed through her mind for the thousandth time. *This was a terrible idea*, Mariah would say. *You should've stayed away. You should've faced your demons years ago, right after Scott …*

She let the ellipsis hang in the air and stepped inside the only bar on Main Street: Jacob's Pub. She wasn't sure who Jacob was but he'd let his business go to hell. The windows were beyond washing, ought to be replaced altogether. There were several booths and tables. An L-shaped bar bordered the drinks and taps. Across the way were two doors: the kitchen and bathroom next to each other.

Faint music played over the speakers. It sounded old and distorted, as if recorded before stereo existed. There were no customers and no one at the bar. Perhaps the business was closed for the night—or for good. Perhaps she ought to leave. Perhaps—

"Can I get you anything, ma'am?"

She jumped at the voice. The man, presumably Jacob, stood in front of her, across the bar. He held an empty glass and she was certain he hadn't been there moments before.

He was probably just stocking something below the bar. People don't just appear out of thin air.

But they do disappear, don't they?

"Ma'am? Everything okay?"

She shook her head. "Yes, I'm sorry. It's been a long day. I'll have whatever's on tap."

"He nodded. All we've got is PBR. Hope that's okay. It may be cheap but it goes down just fine."

She smiled. "PBR sounds good to me."

He smiled back, teeth yellowed with nicotine, beard gray and wiry. "Coming right up." He poured what resembled piss into the glass and slid it over.

Ivy looked through her wallet. "I've only got debit. Do you take plastic?"

He pointed to the sign above the door: *cash only.*

"I'm sorry. Do you have an ATM anywhere?"

"Out back but it's broken. No one ever used it. Never got around to getting it fixed."

She made to leave but he held a hand up. "It's fine. This one's on the house. Besides, you look like you could use a drink. If you don't mind me saying so."

"If you only knew. I appreciate it. I'm staying over at the hotel across the street. I'll use their ATM and be back for more, I'm sure."

His eyebrows lifted. "The hotel, you said? What brings you here?"

She shrugged. "Just passing through."

He laughed. It wasn't a quick chuckle. He held his stomach and howled. A tear or two leaked from his eyes. "That's a good one, Miss."

"What's so funny?"

"It's just that no one *passes through* Marlowe, if you know what I mean." He covered his mouth to block more laughter.

"I'm not sure I do."

His face transitioned quickly to something like concern, maybe even anger. "Lady, I'm sure you know where you are, geographically speaking, but you must also have an inkling as to what happened here."

She sipped before answering and almost spat. The beer was lukewarm and flat, as if it had been sitting out for eons. Particles floated inside the glass, perhaps dust. "Of course I know what happened."

He nodded. "Good. Now that we've got that out of the way, care to share why you're here, in this place, when you could be any other place in the world?"

Because the love of my life is dead and it haunts me every minute of every hour of every day. Because I've seen more imaginary blood than a surgeon sees in his lifetime. Because he told me to come here.

Jacob touched her arm with a skeletal hand. It felt like ice. Her skin grew rigid. "I didn't mean to pry. I know this place inside and out. Whatever your reason for being here is, it can't be for fun. A place like this, where all the good memories have been tarnished by the bad ones … it has a way of calling to you and not the other way around. You catch my meaning?"

She nodded, her mouth frozen open. She caught it loud and clear.

He started to say something else, something that seemed important, but he stopped mid-sentence and scratched his razor wire beard. "Now what were we talking about? That's right! PBR. I got a lot of flack for making it the house beer. Me, I'm not into anything that tastes like apricots or peanut butter or any of that. I want beer that tastes like beer, the kind of thing you can drink and not have to think about it. Know what I mean?"

"I suppose I do." She took another sip, tried to hide the impending gag.

"Now if you'll excuse me," he said, lifting a rack of dingy glasses, "I've got a lot to do. You make yourself at home and holler if you need anything else. Enjoy your stay."

She hadn't quite finished swallowing when he turned around and revealed the axe in his back. It hung at a crooked angle, the top half of the blade buried into his spine, the bottom half sticking out and stained with dark blood. The wound—and come to think of it, his flesh too—was unnatural, as if gangrene had set in long ago but the process had stopped just before full-blown infection. A few flies followed him like begging dogs. He did not notice the axe.

Of course he doesn't. That's because it isn't there to begin with. You're seeing things. Nothing new in that department.

The explanation was fitting but it didn't sit well with her. This seemed different than her normal visions, more ... *realistic* somehow. She wasn't sure how to interpret this development but she didn't intend to stick around.

When the man entered the kitchen, she stood without finishing her beer and left in a hurry.

SEVEN

JUST LIKE THE bar, Hotel Marlowe looked as though it hadn't seen a visitor for decades. The front sidewalk was littered with potholes. The marquee lights were even worse up close. Most were broken and those that remained looked ready to blow at any moment.

Something smelled horrid as Ivy neared the door. She covered her mouth and spotted something in the bushes to her right. She couldn't make out details but the thing had been dead for a while now. Flies buzzed happily over the carcass.

Assuming, of course, the carcass was there to begin with. She couldn't be sure.

She sped through the front doors, not breathing until she was inside, though the air wasn't much better. It wasn't as foul but it wasn't exactly refreshing either. The place smelled of mold and must. The carpet was stained and had long since lost its bounce. The pattern was lost on her, some paisley design that seemed to defy logic.

She assumed she was alone in the front lobby. No one else was dumb enough to come to this cesspool. But when she looked toward the front desk she spotted the man and woman from the rest stop.

The man with the evil eyes, she thought with a shiver.

He pressed the small bell on the counter over and over. "Come on, will you? We've been waiting out here for ten fucking minutes."

The girl squeezed his arm but he batted her away. "It's okay, Zeke. They're probably just busy."

"Busy?" He spun around, his hand pointing in every direction. "Amy, this place doesn't exactly seem hopping, does it?"

"Maybe they're on break or something. Here, come sit down and relax. You're exhausted. We both are."

"Speak for yourself. This is my Disney World and I'll be damned if it's ruined because of shitty service."

From off to the left, another voice spoke. "Why don't you give them a bad Yelp review?" The man, perhaps mid-thirties, with hair and a beard that were prematurely graying caught Ivy's glance and rolled his eyes. "Hope you're not in a hurry." He laughed but she could tell it was forced. He was on edge, looking around every few moments as if he'd find someone watching. On the carpet, in between his feet, lay a large trash bag. He caught her staring and tightened the top, obscuring her view of whatever lay within.

"That's okay," Ivy said. "I can wait."

The man at the counter—Zeke—watched her as she approached. "I'm happy for you, lady. But I'm here on business and I'd like to get started."

"Business?" Ivy said. "What kind of business would take you to Marlowe? If you don't mind me asking?"

He opened his mouth but the girl—Amy—beat him to it. "He's a writer—a journalist. He runs a website about serial killers."

Zeke smiled. His cheeks turned red. "It's nothing really. Killwithathrill.com. Maybe you've heard of it? Especially considering where we are."

Killwithathrill. She spun the words around a few times before she pinpointed them. From her purse she pulled the book she'd bought back in Oregon. "Your little website is in here. I read all about it this morning."

His face beamed, a kid learning he'd won a contest. "In Williamson's book? No way! The guy knows his stuff, interviewed me a while back, but I didn't think I'd make the cut. Figured he'd just focus on Tucker and his family and the—"

"Victims? The ones that bastard slaughtered, you mean? Most of them in this very town? You'd *think* he'd talk about them but this hack focuses more on the killer. It's like Tucker's a superhero instead of psychopath."

"Lady, call him what you want. But that psychopath has thousands of fans and he's paid my rent for the last few years."

"Fans?" She opened the book and, with all the strength she could summon, tore off the cover and several pages before slamming it on the counter. "Here's what I think of his fans. You must be one. I heard you talking about him back at the store like he was Elvis."

His face switched gears. Those eyes, the ones that seemed to belong to someone else, peered toward her. They were equal parts hypnotizing and sinister. "I'm much more than a fan. That's why I'm here."

"What's that supposed to mean?" Ivy said. She tried to sound brave—emphasis on *tried*.

He smiled. "You'll see soon enough."

Amy stepped between them. "Okay, I think everyone's had a long day and we all need to relax."

From behind the counter, a door Ivy hadn't noticed opened.

And out stepped what looked like a ghost.

The girl was no older than twenty-four but she was in rough shape. Her skin was dry and leathery, dark like ash. Her eyes were cavernous and sunken back into her skull, with bruise-like bags circling them, the mark of an insomniac. Her hair had been pulled into a ponytail in a hurry. Several oily strands hung loose.

Around her neck was a red scarf. The longer Ivy looked, the more she suspected it hadn't always been that color. It was stained, moist, like the skin underneath was seeping.

Ivy closed her eyes, took a deep breath, and opened them again.

The girl was still there and she looked just as dead.

"I'm sorry about the wait," she said from behind the counter. "As you might expect, we don't often have visitors these days." She looked toward Zeke and tilted her head. "He'll be so glad to see you've arrived. All of you in fact." She surveyed the rest of the group.

"What the hell's that supposed to mean?" the man with the bag said. "I don't have a reservation. I'm … meeting someone here."

She avoided the question. "My name is Annabelle and I hope

you'll enjoy your stay here. If you need anything—anything at all—don't hesitate to ask. Just know that it may take a while. We've been working with a ghost crew as of late."

"Hey," Zeke said, staring toward the girl. "Don't I know you from somewhere. I swear I've seen you before."

She reached out and touched his hand. He tensed, then eased up. There was something distinctly erotic about his reaction. It was not lost on his girlfriend or wife or whoever she was. Amy sneered.

"Yes," Annabelle said. "I think you do." She cleared her throat, though her voice was just as raspy. Amy got the sense that she hadn't spoken in a long time. "Now if you'll just give me a moment, I'll get your room keys and you'll be on your way."

She turned and fumbled through the rack of keys behind her. The hotel's business practice matched its ancient appearance. There were no computers in sight. Or room cards for that matter. Instead there were elegant keys arranged in numerical order. She grabbed three—106, 107, and 108—and set them down on the desk.

The man with the bag eyed the keys suspiciously. "You mean to tell me we're all staying next to each other?"

Annabelle nodded. "Isn't it wonderful?"

"Wonderful? You said there wasn't anyone else here. So why the hell would you put us so close together?"

Just like Jacob across the street, Annabelle's face turned quickly from that of an angel to that of a devil. "Mr. Roberts, I did not say you were the only guests tonight. I simply said we don't see new guests all that often. Take your key, Ethan, and your bag too. That's why you came here to Marlowe, isn't it?"

The man—Ethan Roberts, apparently—dropped the tough guy veneer. His mouth hung open and he looked just as scared as Ivy felt. "How did you know my name?"

"Like I said before. He's been expecting you."

"He?" Zeke said, cutting in. "As in—"

"Now if you'll excuse me," Annabelle said. "I've some business to attend to. Do you need help with your luggage?"

Ivy looked around at the group. Ethan had only his mystery bag. Amy carried one suitcase, Zeke two, and Ivy hadn't brought anything aside from her purse.

"We'll be fine," Amy said with a smile, trying to ease the tension. It was a lost cause.

Without another word, Annabelle turned around and made her

way back through the door. On her way there, the scarf came loose and, for a moment before she vanished, Ivy spotted an incision that wrapped around most of her neck. White bone peered from within the red, her spinal column, which had been partially snapped.

Ivy wiped away sweat. Just as in Jacob's Pub, this wound, this *blood*, seemed different than from her visions. It seemed real.

She spun around and saw Ethan wearing what she thought was a similar expression. Something akin to fear.

Zeke and Amy were already on their way to the elevators, their key in hand.

Ivy made to ask Ethan if he'd seen the blood but he grabbed his key and hurried along, taking the stairs.

Which left Ivy alone in the lobby of the Hotel Marlowe. She looked at the torn book, still sitting on the front desk, and forced back a wave of nausea. What was it that Annabelle had said earlier? Just before she'd cut Zeke off, she'd said something like—

He's been expecting you.

EIGHT

IN THE STAIRWELL, Ethan stopped long enough to read the note Andrew had left in the glove compartment of the stolen car. It read *Hotel Marlowe, room 107.*

The number matched that of the key he held but it still didn't sit right with him. He wasn't even sure who he was meeting tonight. Andrew had only told him the drop-off would be here at eight o'clock. Ethan looked at his watch and groaned. The damned thing had been fine earlier. In fact, he set it this morning, when sleep had evaded him as it did every morning since Lisa's diagnosis.

Now, the minute and second hands spun in opposite directions. He tapped the screen with his fingers but it did nothing. He couldn't remember what time he'd crossed into Marlowe but he hoped he wasn't running late. He couldn't botch this thing. There was too much at stake.

He imagined Lisa's face this coming Christmas as she stepped into the living room and saw a bare tree, void of any presents. Or, even worse, the piles of medical bills climbing to such a height, his entire family drowned in them.

Ethan shook his head and took the stairs two at a time. There was a tear in the bag, growing quickly. He could see some of the boxes and bottles within, the painkillers painfully obvious within the hole.

He reached the second floor.

Zeke and Amy were entering their room, arguing about something. Ethan couldn't make out the couple's words. Judging by their voices, Amy was scared of whatever Zeke said. The latter, Ethan had noticed, walked around like the world owed him something. It was the same stroll loan applicants used at his day job. A walk of entitlement he saw on a daily basis.

Although there was something else about the guy, wasn't there?

Something that made Ethan's stomach squirm just looking into his eyes.

When they were gone, Ethan stepped into the hall, readied his key, and stopped short at the door.

The other woman came out of the elevator and walked toward her room, on the other side of Zeke's. She nodded toward the bag. "Need help with that?"

He turned it so the tear wasn't visible. "I'm fine."

She faked a smile. "Sorry. I didn't mean to intrude."

He nodded, didn't offer his name. Annabelle had offered it for everyone in the lobby.

Ivy inserted her key, turned the knob. "Can I ask you a question?"

Ethan tensed. "If it's about the bag or why I'm here, then no."

She shook her head. "It's nothing like that. It's just ... that girl downstairs? You saw it too, didn't you? When her scarf came off?"

He swallowed. "I saw something. Looked like an old scar, maybe a tattoo."

"It was more than a scar. It was *bleeding*."

Ethan shrugged. "I guess maybe it was. I didn't stick around long enough to notice. Now if you don't mind ..." He held up his key.

"Not at all. Good luck with ... whatever you're here for."

He nodded. "Yeah, you too."

Another fake smile and she was in the room and closing the door behind her.

Ethan moved quickly, not just because he was so close to the drop-off but because he didn't like being alone in the hall. The shapes from earlier swam on either side of him. They seemed closer now. He was certain if he looked quick enough he'd see something standing there. Something tall and frail and skeletal.

Something a lot like Tucker Ashton.

He opened the door. It was dark inside. He fumbled his way around, feeling for the lamp, until he found the switch and flicked it. Bright light washed over the room and for a moment he was blind.

And in that instant he swore he saw someone sitting in the chair across the way, just next to a desk that looked straight out of a private investigator's office. He covered his eyes and dropped the bag. "Jesus, you scared the shit out of me. I'm Ethan. Andrew's brother? Not sure if I'm late but can we get this over with? It's been a hell of a day."

The figure in the chair did not answer.

Ethan rubbed his eyes and opened them slowly. When the trance wore off, it was replaced by shock.

The chair was empty, though the cushion was indented. He searched the room but there weren't many hiding places. The layout was simple: a bed, a side table, the chair, desk, and a mirror in which he saw his own frightened reflection.

The bathroom then. The guy had gotten spooked. Ethan didn't blame him. Sitting alone, in this room, in this *hotel*—it was enough to make his skin squirm.

He opened the door. The bathroom was cramped and moldy and empty.

Ethan leaned against the wall for a moment, the room doing laps around him.

He was exhausted, on edge. The chair and the room had been empty all along. His mind was playing tricks. Being back in Marlowe had a certain ... effect on him. There was a rational explanation for all of this. He need only to search his mind to find the answer.

The wrong room. That was all. He'd read the slip of paper incorrectly.

He unfolded it again but the words and numerals hadn't changed.

He tossed the bag of pills onto the bed, covered them with the blanket for good measure. For some odd reason, the bulge beneath the fabric seemed humanoid, like there was more than just drugs under there.

He hurried back into the hall, locking the door behind him, and sped downstairs. By the time he reached the front desk, he was winded. Not to mention dehydrated. When was the last time he'd eaten or drank anything? He'd been much too nervous this afternoon, psyching himself up for the heist. Now his stomach gurgled despite his nerves.

He rang the bell but it went unanswered this time. He could see light spilling from underneath the office door and something like a pair of feet standing just on the other side.

"Fuck this," he said as he grabbed his cell and dialed Andrew. And waited for a dial tone that never came. He looked at the screen and nearly tossed the thing. It was malfunctioning somehow. He'd been due for an upgrade for months now. Alexis had been on his back about getting a new one. It would fail the moment he needed it most, his wife had said. That's how these things worked.

There were countless pixels of varying colors and shapes and every few moments it seemed they were ready to form some shape.

He scratched his stubbly cheek and tried to think. Everything about this night seemed wrong. Not just in the failed robbery sort of way. It was deeper than that, less tangible.

It was this *place*. Marlowe was getting to him in a way he couldn't quite comprehend.

He studied the slip of paper for the third time, and though he should've been shocked to find an entirely different address, some part of him had actually *expected* it.

There wasn't a man in his room upstairs because he was at the wrong hotel.

Holiday Inn, Revere, Room 201.

He crumpled the paper and tossed it to the floor, where it scuttled along like a spider.

"Mind if I join you?" the woman said, the one here alone, the one who was transfixed on Annabelle's scar. Or maybe it *had* been an open wound.

Ethan sat in the lounge at one of many tables gathering dust. He waved to the seat across from him. "Be my guest."

She eyed his drink—whiskey sour—and looked around.

"Don't bother," Ethan said. "The bartender seems to have checked out."

"Then how'd you …?"

He sipped and winced at the burn. "I felt entitled on account of the service thus far. You won't tell on me, will you?"

Something like a smile crept across her face. "Only if you don't." She made her way to the bar and poured a generous amount of rum with a dash of coke into a glass. By the time she came back, her glass was nearly half empty. "I'm Ivy," she said between sips. "Ivy Longwood."

"Nice to meet you, Ivy. I'm Ethan."

She nodded. "I know. And so did the girl at the front desk. Which seemed to surprise you a great deal. What brings you to Marlowe?"

He shrugged. "She did seem to know an awful lot about me, didn't she? I'm just passing through. Haven't been here in a long time. Figured I'd catch up on some memories."

"You've been here before then?"

"I used to live here."

She nearly spat her drink out. "Come again?"

He pointed to the rear of the hotel, past the front desk and the sealed door, past the back entrance and toward the streets beyond. "Keep going that way for five or so minutes and you'll wind up on my old street. Skyview Terrace. I'm not sure if the house is still there. Like I said, it's been a long time."

"Were you ... I mean did you live here when it happened?"

"*It* being the massacre?" He shook his head, took a much bigger sip. It didn't burn so much this time. "My family and I moved when I was younger. Tucker wasn't a killer then. At least I don't think so. I tried my best not to watch the trial. It hit too close to home, so to speak, but I did hear that bastard might've already had a few victims before he left home. Wouldn't surprise me. He always had this ... *look* on his face, you know? Like he was thinking terrible things. In hindsight, he probably was."

He thought of that look now. Despite how tired he felt, his mind brought him readily back to his childhood. He was ten again, playing Frisbee with the neighborhood kids in a field off River Road. Dave and Tim and even Andrew (before he grew too cool and long before he was a felon). Standing to the side, watching them play, was a fifth figure. Tucker did not beg to be let into the group, and they wouldn't have let him even if he'd asked. Instead he watched and waited and, perhaps, plotted.

Ethan shivered. It was not from the chill in the hotel lobby.

Ivy's skin turned a certain shade of gray, not unlike Annabelle. "You mean to tell me you knew him?"

He nodded slowly, trying to blink away Tucker's lifeless face. "I guess you could say that, though 'knew' is a strong word. We talked on occasion. Hung out a few times. I didn't give him shit like the others but I didn't exactly invite him into my life with open arms either."

"If I knew that bastard, I'd never step foot here again."

"Believe me, it wasn't my idea. What's with all the questions, anyway? You writing a book?"

"Me? Absolutely not. In case you hadn't heard, they *did* write a book. It came out today, in fact. I started reading it on the plane but I couldn't stomach the thing. He's a killer, not a celebrity, though the author would have you think it's the other way around. And that guy, Zeke? He runs an entire website dedicated to him. I tried to look it up on my phone but the Internet's spotty here."

"More like non-existent." He held up his phone. The screen seemed worse now. He wondered if it would work again after he left Marlowe. "What about you? What brings you to America's favorite murder site?"

"I ..." she trailed off. Her hands fidgeted. She played with a large diamond engagement ring.

"Where's your husband on this fine night?"

She caught him staring and spun her ring around, hiding the diamond from view. "Not here. I mean I'm not married. Or engaged."

"Then why the ring?"

"It's a long story." She finished her drink in one final sip and set it down too hard. "It's getting late. I'm tired."

"Yeah," he said. "Me too. Although, I don't have a clue what time it is."

"There's a clock above the bar."

He stood and stretched. "That doesn't do us much good." Like his watch, the minute and second hands did laps around each other, speeding in opposite directions. It reminded him of a compass in the Bermuda Triangle.

"What's wrong with it?"

"Not sure but they're all that way. I don't think anything works properly in Marlowe. It's like the damned things are scared. I don't blame them one bit. A piece of advice? Whatever you came here for, it's probably not worth it. If I were you, I'd get some sleep and get the hell out of here first thing in the morning. That's my plan."

Ivy watched the clock, her eyes wide, her skin oily with sweat. "I'll take that under advisement." A moment later, she left.

Sitting alone in the bar, Ethan felt a sense of dread so strong it made his skin come alive, every hair standing at attention. He needed to get the hell out of this place but he wasn't about to step foot outside, not while it was dark. He'd told Alexis he had a work conference. Judging by her reaction, she hadn't bought his cover story but she didn't press the issue either. She wouldn't come searching if he didn't answer his phone. Not tonight, at least. Which meant he was unaccounted for. If anything were to happen to him, no one would know where he really was. Not even Andrew, on account of the note magically changing addresses.

He nearly jogged to his room, keeping his eyes steady, not looking in any direction other than forward, telling himself the dread he felt was nothing more than nerves.

Morning could not come soon enough.

NINE

AMY WASN'T DREAMING. Not in the traditional sense, at least. Her mind was tired, as was her body, but it refused to shut off entirely. She was in a transitional state, inches away from sleep but still tethered to reality.

She lay on her back, staring at the moldy ceiling. There was a stain up there. It had been smaller when they first checked in. She was sure of it. In the last hour it had grown, changing shapes as it expanded. She watched it like a cloud, trying to pinpoint an image. Each new transformation brought with it a jolt, her blood pressure spiking. She saw teeth and glowing eyes and something like a face peering down at her.

Perhaps something was dripping through the floor of the room upstairs but surely no one was up there. The girl at the desk—Annabelle—must have been lying when she'd said there were other guests. The hotel, much like the town itself, seemed abandoned.

Her prickly skin and speeding pulse begged to differ, quite certain they were not alone. The others, whoever they may be, were just good at staying hidden.

She tensed, tried to force her thoughts elsewhere, though where they landed wasn't much better. She recalled her first weeks living in Virginia. She stayed in a small apartment with a roommate—Tanya—who'd barely spoken during their entire time together. The girl never seemed to be home. She majored in nursing at the same college, worked well into the night. Amy had hoped they could be friends but after only a few days of the living situation, she knew it wasn't meant to be.

In fact *no* friends seemed meant to be. Her classmates all had their own cliques. Whenever she reached out she was shot down. It felt like high school all over again. Except she hadn't felt this alone in high school. She hadn't been the most popular girl in her class but she'd had *some* friends.

After she received The Call, the one where she'd been certain her mother was dead, she'd drifted away from just about every person in her life. Her biological father had died when she was five. One day he was healthy, the next he suffered a stroke and died hours later. Her stepfather, Grant, was a stranger. Much like Tanya, they may have lived together but they weren't friends and certainly not family.

So Amy had chosen a state at random—Virginia, as it turned out—and traveled from Florida to her new home and school. She lost touch with her old friends and failed to make new ones. It was lonely to say the least.

Until she'd met Zeke.

She felt him stir in his sleep as if hearing his name. Earlier, he'd insisted they explore the town. He was looking for something, he told her, though he wouldn't tell her what. She'd begged him to take the night off. He was exhausted, even if he wasn't aware. He'd fought her until he fell asleep an hour ago.

She watched his sleeping face. She'd wanted to leave him for months now. Her loneliness had been the culprit of their relationship and now she felt trapped. Worse still, she was *afraid* to leave him. He'd been growing stranger in recent times. She couldn't be certain how he'd react. Now that they were in Marlowe, on his dream vacation, she couldn't bring the subject up. Not yet, at least.

But what if you never had another chance?

Shivering, she tried to make sense of the question but she froze when Zeke mumbled something in his sleep and stood. It was obvious by the way he stumbled that he was sleepwalking again. He whispered words as if in mid-conversation with someone she couldn't see. Whatever they spoke of, it excited him.

He sat at the desk and wrote something in his notebook. Another note. When he was finished, he stood again and stepped into the hallway.

She did not want to follow him. While he may have been asleep, he moved like he had a destination in mind. No, that wasn't quite right. It was more like he was a *puppet*, like someone—some*thing*—held the strings.

But she couldn't let him wander off. They weren't in the safety of their home. There were staircases and balconies. He could get himself hurt.

She got out of bed and, on her way out of the room, glanced at the newest note.

And wished she hadn't.

The words were written in such a rush, they looked more like symbols. Their message, though, was quite clear. It was another letter, as she'd suspected. Just like the rest, he'd written the words as if they weren't from him but someone else.

Tucker Ashton.

Dear Zeke,

It's almost time now. We're so close. You're still on board, right? Of course you are. You've always been on board. You may not realize this but we share a special bond, you and I. We think the same way. And right now, we've never been closer. I'll be waiting at the end of the first floor hall. The door would have you think it's a utility room but don't believe your eyes. Marlowe is my town now. It has a way of bending to my command. You must hurry, though. We don't have much time. It's complicated but you'll have to trust me. I'm back, Zeke, and I'm going to make you a millionaire. We'll be legends together.

Your Old Pal Tucker.

Amy tried to block the gasp but it was insistent, spilling out of her mouth as she dropped the note. It landed on the carpet and leaned against the desk's leg so the words still faced her. Like they demanded to be read.

She peered into the hall and caught the sight of Zeke's jet-black hair as he rounded the corner and made his way, presumably, to the utility room.

Unless you went by the letter's instructions. In which case, it wasn't a utility room at all. Which made it ... what?

She didn't have an answer. Didn't *want* an answer. She paced for a moment before making a decision. She'd go after Zeke but only to ensure he didn't get hurt. When he was tucked back in and dreaming of his favorite serial killer, she'd pack her things and hit the road. If she couldn't tell him things were over, for fear of his reaction, then she wouldn't.

The letter fluttered as if from a breeze, though both windows were closed.

She stepped into the hall and hurried, hoping she could catch Zeke before he made it to the mystery room. She wasn't sure what lay inside, but something told her if Zeke entered, he would not come out the same.

"Damn thing," Ivy said for the thousandth time. Her phone was acting strangely. Earlier there'd been no Internet connection and now, when she tried to call Mariah, it didn't work at all. She dialed her sister's number again and held the phone to her ear.

There was no ring tone, nor static, but there *was* something. Something like breathing.

She shook her head. *You're being ridiculous. It's just this place and that guy—Ethan's—story. If you believe him, then this entire town is ... what? Haunted?*

For a moment, the slight hissing (breathing) grew louder in her ear. She tossed the phone across the room. It landed on the bed, screen side up, and even from her spot near the bathroom she could see the screen as it transitioned from her wallpaper (a picture of her and Scott, of course) to something that looked very much like a computer just before it crashes. Pixels and lines with no semblance of a pattern.

It felt wrong not being able to see Scott's face smiling at her. It was a constant comfort. Every time she turned her phone on, she felt a bit calmer. Her therapist insisted it was a step back in her road to closure but if it held off a panic attack or ten, she saw nothing wrong with leaving the wallpaper as is.

She nibbled her nails and tried to think. Wasn't there a phone downstairs in the lobby? Had Ethan mentioned if he'd tried it or if it worked? She didn't like the idea of going back down there, of being in the same room as Annabelle and her severed spine. Ivy thought it was just one of her hallucinations until she'd seen the way Ethan stared. He'd shrugged it off but she could tell they were on the same page.

But Mariah would worry. She'd made Ivy promise to call her the moment she checked in. And that hadn't been the only promise, had it?

Promise you'll get the hell out of there if something goes wrong.

Ivy wasn't sure if any of this counted as wrong but it certainly *felt* that way. She'd do as Ethan said, wait it out until morning and then get the hell out of this black hole the moment the sun was in the sky. If her phone worked once she got back to civilization, then all the better. If not, she'd use the one at the convenience store, tell her sister she'd been right all along.

Ivy caught herself twirling the engagement ring around her finger, the one Ethan had asked about. The one she sometimes forgot she wore in the first place.

The one she found while cleaning out Scott's bureau.

After … *that night* … she'd delayed going through his belongings. To do so would be to admit he was really gone. To believe she really *had* seen his corpse, really *had* seen the message written in his blood and addressed, she assumed, to her.

I'll be seeing you.

She'd made hints during their relationship, of course. What woman didn't when they found The One? They rarely fought and when they did something came from it. A behavior was changed, an apology given. It was, by all counts, the healthiest relationship she'd ever been in. When the ring didn't come after her initial hints, she thought: *That's fine. He loves me and he's here, so what's it matter if we don't make it official just yet?*

Part of her was disappointed, sure, but she'd never stopped believing he loved her. He made that apparent every chance he had. He was a good man. The kind of person you only meet once in your life. The kind that, despite being an inch shorter than you, doesn't feel the need to prove his masculinity. The kind that seems cool and calm during times of crisis. It was that latter quality she missed so much now. Had he been here with her, he would've known what to do, would've stroked her hair and told her to breathe slowly.

But you're forgetting if he was here, you wouldn't be in Marlowe. You'd be back home in Portland, sipping wine by the fire or eating his world famous meat loaf instead of losing your mind in what is probably the most haunted place in the country.

Her thoughts went on, stuttering in her mind. She tried to make them stop but it was a lost cause. They kept on until the moment she heard the knock at the door.

It was a loud thud, strong enough to shake the door in its frame. Yet it wasn't demanding to be let in. It simply wanted her to know it was there.

It? Was she still thinking about the knock or who (what) was on the other side?

It came again, louder this time. Three quick, strong thuds.

Her voice shook and she was shocked it worked at all. "W-who is it?"

A long pause. She could hear something out there, something like the heavy breathing she'd heard on the phone.

Finally, when the voice came, she nearly screamed. "Room service." It was raspy and high-pitched, a teenage girl mixed with an elderly woman.

Her skin crawled with warnings. "I didn't order anything. You must have the wrong room."

A pause, followed by three more knocks. The door shook worse this time. Would it be easy to break down?

"Room service." The individual giggled under their breath as if trying to hide a prank, but something told her pranks didn't exist in this town. There was nothing funny about Marlowe.

"Please," Ivy said. "I didn't order anything. I'm very tired and I'd like to sleep."

Three final knocks. She thought she heard the wood splintering. "Room service." Another giggle, then footsteps down the hall. It sounded as if they skipped along the way.

Ivy waited an eternity before she opened her purse and grabbed her pepper spray. She opened the door, tensing, certain she'd see the owner of the knocks. And even more certain it would not be human.

Peeking her head into the hall, she saw nothing aside from the metal tray on the carpet in front of her. An elegant cover had been placed over the plate, like something in a four-star hotel. She wasn't certain how many stars Hotel Marlowe had earned but the cover felt out of place. Not to mention she really hadn't ordered anything.

She kneeled down and reached for the cover's handle despite her internal warnings, her mind begging her to stop. She held on for a long time before she lifted it and almost fainted at the sight of the two objects.

The first was a spider much bigger than she'd ever seen. It was covered in fur. Its legs were long and thick and its eyes seemed to study her for a moment, as if wondering if she was worth the effort of jumping and biting. She was certain it was poisonous, judging by the fang-like teeth protruding from its lips.

But oddly enough, the spider wasn't what worried her the most. It eventually grew bored and scuttled down the hallway.

The second object was, in a way, just as poisonous.

The skeletal face watched her from below, begging her to pick the book up and open its cover, which she did with a hypnotic reach of her hand. It wasn't her copy of *Birth of a Monster*. The binding looked brand new, no signs of tearing.

A joke. It had to be a joke. That asshole Zeke was playing tricks with her. But the theory didn't ring true in her thoughts.

She opened the book and chose a passage at random.

And felt like crying when she read:

Ivy Longwood is a dumb little bitch who thinks the world owes her something just because her husband—shorter than her, mind you (how pathetic is that?)—got hacked up in his bathroom while she was out with the girls. She thinks she's the only one who's ever faced tragedy. Her sister, Mariah, considers kicking Ivy out every night. What's the sense in keeping her around if Ivy is just going to play the dead boyfriend card every chance she gets? Ivy doesn't pay rent or help with the chores. She doesn't do much of anything except sulk all day. Then she became obsessed with the message. The one written in her midget boyfriend's blood. It said I'll be seeing you *and now that she's in Marlowe, in the belly of the beast, it's more than true. It's inevitable. And when she does see me, I'm going to do her sister a favor. I'm going to cut her stupid limbs and stupid nipples and stupid head right off her body.*

She dropped the book. It landed words-side up. The pages moved, the next chapter presenting itself but she did not read further. Instead she opened her mouth and attempted to scream.

But it was cut off by *another* scream. One that came from down the hall. It sounded familiar.

Amy.

TEN

ETHAN WAS HAVING trouble sleeping. Nothing new there.

The last six months had been spent mostly awake, in a zombie-like state that left him spacing out for much of the day. At work, in between filling out forms and interviewing loan applicants, he would stare out the window. His bank was located off I-95 and his office faced the traffic. Each day he had the most perfect view of rush hour, the impending clusterfuck he'd face on his ride home. And when he finally *got* home, usually an hour and a half later, he'd have just enough time to eat dinner with Alexis and Lisa before heading back out the door to the gas station for his night shift.

He did it all with a smile, pretended it was no big deal. Made like nothing was wrong and he wasn't giving himself an ulcer from the stress and the bad thoughts that reminded him just because Lisa was responding to the treatment didn't mean she was out of the woods yet.

These latter thoughts spun through his mind now, amplified by Hotel Marlowe. Every time he closed his eyes, he'd see his daughter's beautiful face, drained of color. Drained of life. Lying in a casket, her green eyes closed forever. The princess had finally lost the battle against the dragon.

Ethan opened his eyes and wiped away moisture. Something told him it wasn't his allergies.

As silly as it seemed, he'd unfolded Lisa's drawing and laid it out on the bed next to him. He would not admit to himself how scared he was to be back home. Nor would he acknowledge the nagging suspicion things were about to get much worse. But with the picture inches away, he was able to breathe a bit easier.

Except when he reached across the bed and felt for the wrinkled piece of paper, he felt nothing but the sheet. His pulse sped. He searched under the pillows, under his body, then tore off the covers and fitted sheet. There was only a stained mattress. In the dim light of the room, the stain looked very dark. He had the feeling if he reached out, it would feel warm, like something had crawled into the inner workings and died recently.

But he was less concerned about the stain than he was the drawing. It may have been just a slip of paper but to him it was more than that. To him it was his amulet, the only weapon he had in this hell he'd traveled to.

"Looking for this?"

The voice came from behind. It was calm and collected and it brought with it a cool draft that sent every inch of Ethan's skin into a frenzy. His joints froze.

"She's talented, isn't she?" the voice said. "When I was her age, I couldn't draw a stick figure worth a shit. But this—it's not half bad. The castle's a bit off but she's just a kid, I suppose. And that dragon—man, that dragon. It's creepy, you know? Gives me the heebie-jeebies. And that's saying something, all things considered."

Ethan forced his mouth open. "You're not here."

"Come again?"

"You're not here, in this room with me, because you're dead."

"From where I'm sitting, I can promise you that's a lie. I would know if I was dead. Do I *look* dead to you?"

Though his sanity begged him to stay frozen, Ethan broke his paralysis and spun around. A figure sat in the chair, the one he'd seen earlier for the briefest of moments. The one he'd thought was Andrew's liaison.

The room was black save for the small nightlight in the corner. It cast enough light so that the figure's features were partially visible: yellowed teeth and thin lips, a witch-like chin and pronounced Adam's apple. But the eyes—they remained hidden and for that Ethan was thankful.

Tucker Ashton smiled. "It's been a long time."

Ethan shook his head, swallowed back bile. "You can't be here. You'd have to be crazy to come back to this place after what you did."

"You know I never really liked that word. *Crazy*. It sounds so harsh. I don't think most people understand its meaning. They use it too freely, apply it to anything they don't quite understand. You see a homeless guy with shit-stained pants, mumbling to himself about the end of days, you call him crazy. You see a guy holding a sign that says something about lizard people, about every politician secretly being an alien—crazy. You hear some kid in a tiny town killed a bunch of people and uploaded it all onto the Internet and what do you say?"

"Crazy," Ethan answered.

"See, there it is again. None of this is crazy. It's all very real and I'm not dead. You must have known all along, deep down inside of that little noggin of yours, that I was out there. I may have gone somewhere, someplace that's as far from reality as possible, but I came *back*. And that's another word that always leaves a bad taste in my mouth. Reality. It sounds so contrived." He held up Lisa's drawing, the top of it pinched between his thumbs and index fingers.

"You wouldn't dare," Ethan said through gritted teeth.

"What if I told you your little girl is going to die either way, that it doesn't matter how much money you thought you'd bring home? That all the medicine in the world couldn't save her? Not that you'd see her shrivel anyway. You won't be going home. *This* is your home now—again. Except this isn't the Marlowe you remember. It's *my* Marlowe. And in this place, you can't stop the dragon, Ethan. Because I *am* the fucking dragon."

Tucker tore a small section of the paper. Ethan winced, could actually feel it, like the drawing was part of him. In a way, he thought, it was.

Tucker laughed and dropped the picture. It floated to the floor near his feet. "I'm just getting started. I've got such plans for you and your friends." He opened his mouth and his voice changed. He let forth a shrill, high-pitched scream that did not match his timbre.

From the hall came slamming fists on the door. "Ethan, open up. It's Ivy. Amy's in trouble. It's that bastard boyfriend of hers."

When Ethan looked back toward the chair, it was empty. No indentations on the fabric, no proof it had been occupied in the first place.

Aside from the tiny tear in the top of Lisa's drawing.

Ethan placed it back into his wallet, opened the door, and followed Ivy down the hall. In a way, the distraction was a blessing.

Because if he'd stopped to consider what he'd just witnessed, even for a moment, he'd lose what little sanity he had left.

Zeke followed the note's instructions to a tee. He rounded the hallway and, sure enough, at the end was a door marked *utility room*. At first glance it was nothing special but as the letter had explained, you couldn't always believe your eyes. Sometimes it was what rested beneath the surface that mattered.

He walked as if in a dream, though he was certain he was awake. He felt cool air on his skin, drying away his sleep sweat. The door called to him, a soothing voice begging him onward. He felt his sweat pants pockets, realized he hadn't brought his laptop or camera, no pen or paper. But none of that mattered. Whatever was behind that door, it was more than just an interview. It was a dream come true.

From behind, he heard Amy's voice calling. She'd never get to him in time. She was a good girl, someone he truly cared for. His attraction had been purely physical at first. Her tits were geometrically perfect, filled his hands in just the right way. And she could fuck for hours on end, never growing tired until they both passed out with their hearts racing. But it had evolved past that. At one point, he'd seen a future with her: kids, a house—all of it.

Now, though, he realized it was just a fantasy. He could hold those miraculous tits all he wanted, watch her pretty little face as she slept for hours on end, but she ultimately came second. He couldn't let her get in the way of this moment to end all moments.

He reached for the door, touched the knob. It was warm, inviting. It turned without effort, opened with ease. Inside, the light was blinding. Studio lights, he realized. When his eyes adjusted he saw video cameras and the cue cards, the audience and microphones, but more importantly he saw two chairs positioned in the middle of it all. The farthest was empty, facing Zeke, but the closest, the one that faced away—it was quite full.

Even from behind, Zeke could spot Tucker easily. His red hair and freckled neck, so thin it resembled a snake. He turned his head so one eye faced Zeke. "I was beginning to worry you wouldn't show up."

Zeke swallowed. His throat was swollen. His skin was on fire.

"Don't be bashful." Tucker raised a hand and waved him on.

This is it, Zeke thought. *You're about to meet your hero, the most infamous killer of them all. And here, in this utility-closet-turned-television-studio, in the heart of Hotel Marlowe, no one is here to judge. No one will call you sick or disturbed. No one will berate you and your "hobby." Because here it's more than a hobby. More than a job.*

It's your life.

He nodded. It sounded wonderful. No one had ever understood his fascination with serial killers. It started in high school, when one of his teachers mentioned Ed Gein in passing. He'd done research that night instead of writing a paper on the industrial revolution. A lifelong obsession was born.

His parents hadn't gotten it either. Reading about such morbid things, his mother insisted, was not healthy. But he'd never hurt anyone with his studies or, later, his career. He simply presented the facts, no matter how *morbid* those facts may have been.

And all of it had been leading up to this.

He made his way toward the empty chair, studied the studio to delay the moment when he finally set eyes on his hero. The audience seats were full but he couldn't see any of the audience *members*. They were shrouded in shadows, the bright lights not shining in their direction. Still, he could sense them watching. Waiting.

"Well? Are we still on for our interview?"

Zeke locked eyes with Tucker Ashton. *The* Tucker Ashton. He took a deep breath, steadied his shaking hands. There was nothing to be nervous about. They'd spoken through letters, after all. This was no different. Yeah, right.

Tucker wore white pants, white blazer and shirt, white shoes and tie—everything white. He caught Zeke staring at his outfit and shrugged. "Oh, this?" He looked around and lowered his voice. "Blood looks so … *vibrant* on white, wouldn't you agree?"

Zeke nodded, his eyes just as wide as that first night of research.

"And between you and me, I plan on seeing a lot of blood tonight. That's why I need your help. But I'm sure you must have some questions first."

"Too many. I could ask hundreds, maybe thousands. I've been

waiting for this—"

"All your life," Tucker finished. "I know. Ask away. I've got to warn you, though. We don't have all that much time. There'll be plenty of opportunities for questions later. For now, how about one?"

"Anything?"

"Anything."

Zeke searched thoughts and memories. He'd fantasized of this moment countless times, had a mock questionnaire in his desk at home, among his collection. But now, put on the spot, his mind drew a blank. He asked the first thing that rolled onto his tongue. "Why did you come back?"

"To Marlowe, you mean?"

"Yes. Why come back to the place where you were caught? Doesn't it seem a bit risky?"

Tucker smiled. He looked much paler in real life. His skin was nearly translucent, the blue veins beneath bulging like tumors. "I guess it would be risky if I wasn't in control. You'd have to be crazy to come back here after killing so many people. This is the scene of the *crime*, man. Where the shit went down. But, see, I didn't come back to Marlowe. At least not the one you've seen on television or read about in books. Speaking of which, have you read the newest one? Reads like a love letter. Poor Charles. He wanted to write something that condemned me. But that kind of stuff doesn't sell. People want the same thing I do. They want blood. If they didn't, if people truly were good and decent, then why did I have so many views on my videos? People ate them up like it was porn, just a few images to add to the spank bank for later. But I digress. The reason I came back to Marlowe was to make it my own. It's like I said before. This isn't the same town I grew up in. It's a new place. A place to start over, to build a kingdom. And you, Zeke, are one of the last pieces of the puzzle."

Zeke said nothing. Mostly because he hadn't understood a word of Tucker's diatribe. At least not on a conscious level. Some part of him, though, some deep and dark chamber of his mind, got the message loud and clear.

There was something special happening in Marlowe.

And Zeke had a VIP ticket to the show.

"Now," Tucker said. "You can ask me the rest later. We've got to get moving."

"Where are we going?" Zeke's eyes veered toward the audience. Now that he'd adjusted to the lights, he could make out some of the faces in the front row. They were just as pale as Tucker but that's where the comparison ended. Many were missing limbs and eyes, with open wounds bleeding freely onto the seats. The last sane part of his mind sounded a warning. Something was terribly wrong about all this. Just as soon as the warning sounded, it was gone, replaced by Tucker's voice.

"We need to take care of that girlfriend of yours. She's easy on the eyes but she's trouble. She'll only get in our way. I'm sure you understand."

Zeke nodded, a reflex.

"Good. Let's get on with it then. She should be showing up in …" He lifted a sleeve of his suit and stared at his bony wrist, at the spot where a watch would've been, had there been one. "Three, two, one."

The door crashed open.

Amy ran into the studio but froze halfway to the seats. She held a hand up, blocking out the harsh lights, and stared into the audience.

And screamed.

ELEVEN

UP AHEAD, IVY saw Amy's blond hair and bare legs. She wore a tank top and gym shorts. After screaming for what seemed like forever, she fell unconscious onto the floor. With what lay within the utility room in plain view, Ivy saw why.

It wasn't that asshole boyfriend of hers, watching Ivy like she was a piece of meat. It wasn't the television studio mere feet away instead of mops and brooms and rubber gloves. It wasn't even the bloodied audience members, most of them looking very much like walking corpses.

No, Amy had fainted because of the skeleton in the white suit.

Tucker Ashton stood from his seat, turned around, and smiled. "Ivy, I'm so glad you could make it. I was worried you were having second thoughts. Or your sister would convince you to stay behind. But we both know what she *really* wants. You read about it, after all. Tell me, did you like the book? I had it sent to your room, compliments of the chef." He winked. She shivered. "Deep down, we both know your sister is praying you don't come back. You're more burden than family."

The hotel swayed. Her feet turned to gelatin, the floor to quicksand. She would sink forever, pulled down into some dark place miles beneath Hotel Marlowe.

She nearly followed Amy's example before the arms stopped her from falling. She tensed, spun around, certain it was Tucker. He was everywhere at once.

She saw it was just Ethan, the man with the bag. *What's in the bag, anyway?* she almost asked. She laughed instead, feeling lightheaded.

She closed her eyes, got her second wind. Scott was there, burned into the back of her lids. His corpse, his shredded clothes, his torn skin. And the blood, how it had soaked into her, even though she hadn't come in contact with it. It had followed her, haunted her worse than any ghost or spirit.

In the span of a moment, Ivy went from a dizzy widow to feral lion. She gritted her teeth, faced the impossible room, and made to sprint inside.

Ethan held her back. "We have to go. We have to grab Amy and go."

She shook her head. "That bastard took everything from me. I'm taking it back."

"It's suicide."

"So is this place. This entire town. We should've never come here."

"You can say that again." He held tighter as she fought harder. "If you run into that room, you're dead. What good does that do?"

"What's it matter?"

"It matters because that fucker already killed too many innocent people. He doesn't deserve more."

From the studio came a giggle. "What are we chatting about? What's so important?" Tucker had moved closer to the door. "Do I seem real enough now that I'm not in the shadows, Ethan? Do you believe I've come back? I regret not tearing up that picture of yours. There's still time, though."

"What's he talking about?" Ivy said, struggling to break Ethan's grip.

"Nothing. Don't listen to a word he says. He gets into your head."

"I may be a killer," Tucker said, "but I'm no brainwasher. I didn't make anyone watch those videos. I bet you watched a few yourself. Just to see what all the hubbub was about. You wanted to believe the blood was just corn syrup and food coloring but you knew the moment you started watching it was real. And the best part? You *knew* the killer. Grew up on the same street. Would you like my autograph?"

Ethan whispered into Ivy's ear. "When I let go, turn around and head for the stairs. I'm grabbing Amy and we're getting the hell out of here. Got it?"

Ivy almost argued but thought better of it. He was right. Tucker did have a way of getting into your head. She could almost feel him there, crawling through her memories, using them against her.

Ethan tightened his grip. "Got it?"

She nodded, watched the way Tucker stood above Amy. Observing her unconscious form. She did not want to imagine his train of thought but the way he stared—it was as if he was framing a shot for his next video.

And Amy was the star.

"Go," Ethan yelled into her ear. She spun around and headed for the stairs, telling herself she'd nodded off in bed. This was all just a bad dream. The nightmare to end all nightmares. Her shrink would have a field day.

In the corner of her eye, she saw movement. It could've been Ethan, Amy dangling over his shoulder, or it could've been Tucker himself chasing after her.

Listen to yourself. This all sounds so crazy. So unbelievably, fucking insane.

But it was real. That was the worst part. It wasn't like the everyday blood, wasn't some delusion tied into her grieving process.

She reached the front door and gagged when the scent hit her nostrils. The dead thing from earlier still lay in the same spot. Whatever it had been in life was now a bloated, decaying mess. Hundreds more flies buzzed over the carcass, feasting.

Ivy turned her head and vomited into the bushes, all of them bare, as if fall had come months early. Her throat burned. She hadn't eaten since the plane. The only things in her stomach were the beer and rum. She wiped her mouth and heard footsteps.

"Did you say you drove here?" It was Ethan. Amy wasn't hanging off his shoulder but she *was* in his arms. He carried her like a bride on her wedding night.

Some wedding, Ivy thought as she pointed across the street to the PT Cruiser.

Ethan nodded and jogged. She followed suit. For a panicked moment she was certain she'd forgotten the keys back in her room, but she felt her pockets and detected their shape. She'd always kept a key on her. Just in case. Mariah said it was paranoia, that Ivy didn't trust anyone or anything after Scott …

But her paranoia proved useful as she reached the car and unlocked the doors.

Ethan tossed Amy into the backseat. She was still out cold, murmuring something in her sleep. Ivy hoped her dream wasn't any worse than this. She started the car and backed out of the space.

Tucker and Zeke had not followed them but the door to Hotel Marlowe was not empty. A shape stood out front. Ivy squinted and saw the girl from the front desk. Annabelle waved and smiled like she was wishing them a happy rest of their vacation.

The girl unwrapped her scarf, revealing the wound in question from earlier, though there was no longer any question. With both hands, she lifted her head from its resting spot. It came loose with ease and she held it out like a gift. Her detached face blew them a kiss. The severed spine wriggled on its own accord, the movement like that of a worm or slug.

"Let's get the fuck out of this town," Ethan said from the passenger seat.

"That's the smartest thing you've said all night." Ivy pushed the pedal as far as it would go. The car skidded for a moment before straightening out and taking off toward the rural road she'd traveled hours earlier. In the rearview, Main Street and Annabelle faded. For some odd reason, though, Ivy felt like they were being followed. "Do you see anything back there?"

Ethan turned around, shook his head. "Nothing."

"Do you think we lost them?"

He shrugged, tried to catch his breath. "How should I know? They don't seem to be playing by the rules of reality."

"Fair point."

They drove in silence for minutes that felt more like hours.

"How much longer?" she finally said.

"It should be just up ahead. You'll see a convenience store."

She nodded. "I know the place."

The trees cleared in the distance. The back of the graffitied sign came into view, then the store. She saw someone stepping out of its entrance. The bearded man from earlier who'd been embarrassed by his bubble blowing skills. She'd never been happier to see someone. She'd pull over, tell him to call the cops, and offer to buy him all the gum in the world.

"Stop!" Ethan said.

She slammed the brakes. The car screeched, throwing sparks onto the road.

Up ahead, a yard or so before the welcome sign, stood a gouge in the earth. It had not been there earlier. Now, though, it looked like an earthquake had rumbled through Marlowe. She was certain the car would skid into the hole. She closed her eyes, stopped breathing.

When she opened them again, the Cruiser was still, inches from the gap. She couldn't see how far down it reached but something told her it was deep.

"What the hell …" Ethan said as he stepped outside.

Ivy parked and followed him. The crack was impossibly deep and wide. She looked left and right. It stretched for miles in either direction. "This isn't real. It can't be."

Ethan picked up a rock, tossed it in. It fell forever, until blackness covered it.

There was no sound of it hitting the bottom, no sign there *was* a bottom. Could that be true? Could something come up from behind and push her into this newly formed hole? Could you truly fall forever?

Yes, you can. You've been falling for years with no sign of hitting the bottom.

The man from the store was locking up and stepping into his car. Ivy and Ethan waved their hands and shouted for his attention.

He paid them no notice.

Jack Larson had owned A to Z Convenience for most of his life. His father had bought the place from a man named Sadaf. Jack had only fleeting memories of the guy but he'd been nice enough, slipped him a few free sticks of gum every now and then. He hadn't deserved the racial slurs people—his father included—threw his way. He'd been the only man of Middle Eastern descent in the area and as such had been treated like an oddity. It had been Jack's introduction to how cruel the world could be.

Now that he'd run the store for the better part of thirty years, though, he knew it was much worse than he'd initially thought.

Take the store's location, for example. He saw that damned Marlowe sign every morning and night. It served as a reminder of what had happened, hundreds of innocent people losing their lives just because some nut job liked to film his atrocities. Jack had never watched any of the videos himself but he'd heard of them at plenty of bars, college kids talking about the screams and the pleas as if they were just bad horror movies and Tucker Ashton was no more than an urban legend.

That is, until he came back to his hometown and went on a night-long killing spree. Then he dropped the "urban" and became a full-on legend. As sick as it seemed, that bastard was a celebrity around here, a black cloud that had settled over the surrounding towns. Now there was a book out, probably a movie next.

And Jack had had quite enough. He'd been toying with the idea of selling the shop, moving down to Florida. Hell, he could probably open up a new store and make twice the money. Property was cheap, the weather preferable, and he wouldn't have to see that sign every time he glanced out the window.

Last stop.

He locked the door behind him, triple-checked it as his father had shown him just before the heart attack got him. Truthfully, it didn't matter. No matter how tight you locked up, if someone wanted to break in, they could do so with ease. But out here, so close to Marlowe, it was never an issue. Hardly anyone traveled this road, unless you counted the pretty lady from earlier, the one that had made his bubble pop. His face reddened. Good thing he was alone.

Then there was the couple. The guy talking about Tucker a mile a minute, the girl looking like she wanted to run for the hills. Jack considered himself a good judge of character after dealing with the public for decades. That kid's character was rotten. There was something off about him Jack couldn't quite pinpoint. Probably better that way.

He took one last look at the shop, peered through the glass to ensure no one moved inside, a forgotten customer or clever thief.

Or something worse.

He shivered, pulled up his collar against the spring breeze.

On his way to the truck he froze. For a brief moment, he thought he saw something in his periphery, some undefined movement. He didn't want to look. The night played tricks and out here, geographically speaking, it did more than that. He'd seen plenty of inexplicable things. Shadows and shapes that were unaccounted for.

Against his will, he turned his head as he slid the key into the door. For a nanosecond, he thought he saw two figures standing in the middle of the road. Waving at him, as if for help. In fact, if he listened closely, he could hear their voices, though the words were muffled.

He let go of the key, stepped into the road, and rubbed his eyes. The air shimmered, filled with something like a charge. He hadn't caught the weather forecast, wasn't sure if a storm was coming. The way the hair on his arms stood to sharp points, though—that was evidence enough.

He squinted once more and saw the shapes were gone, as were the voices. There was nothing down that road but darkness. He jogged toward the truck, didn't want to be caught outside when the storm finally arrived, though this was only half true.

The other half, he thought as he blew a bubble, this one stopping just before it exploded onto his chin, was simple yet embarrassing.

There may have only been darkness down that road but it felt otherwise.

It felt like the darkness had eyes. Eyes that never blinked and never tired.

He sped off in the opposite direction, the tires kicking up clouds of dust and, mercifully, obscuring the rearview mirror.

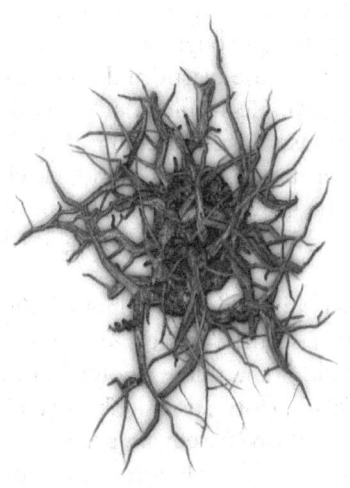

The following excerpts were taken from Charles Williamson's *Birth of a Monster*, published on the day of his death.

Later, after the road trip and eventual hometown rampage, Tucker Ashton would tell authorities he learned to kill from the shadows. He spoke of them, of darkness in general, as though it were alive. Something tangible that breathed and lived and gave detailed instructions on how to hunt victims. The half dozen therapists that interviewed Tucker during his imprisonment came to the same theory: for him, the dark had become his friend. During those lonely nights, after the sun had set and night covered the basement, he would stare deep into the shadows for hours. Eventually he came to believe the shadows stared back.

And then there was the issue of the potatoes.

Tucker was not sure where they came from. Perhaps his father, in a drunken stupor (becoming more and more routine after the death of his wife) had wandered into Tucker's room while he slept and dropped them off. Usually he slid a plate of food onto the top step, something partially microwaved: pizza rolls or Hot Pockets.

According to Tucker, they were always cold in the middle.

He noticed the potatoes one evening, just before the sun had set enough to shroud his living quarters in shadows. They lay in the corner, within a crinkled plastic bag. He wasn't sure how long they'd been there but it was long enough so that they'd grown. Several stalks had pierced through the plastic and grew upward. The transformation fascinated him. He would wait patiently all through the night (he'd developed insomnia, something that likely aided his descent into madness) for the sun to finally show itself. He would note the development of the growth until, finally, the stalk reached epic proportions. It climbed to several feet, hanging firmly against the wall like a vine.

While under observation, Tucker admitted his fascination. He drew a conclusion that seemed to be more of a revelation. Some things grew in the dark. Some things evolved in the shadows. Like the potatoes and their transformation, he believed he was becoming something else in that dusty basement chamber. He believed the shadows and his computer (his only form of escape) were both part of his metamorphosis.

After he left, police searched the Ashton residence. They found the potatoes in the corner of the basement, just where Tucker had left them. The vines had grown nearly to the ceiling. They stank of mold and rot, much like the scene of his many murders. Before Tucker had gone on his trip, a few weeks before his eighteenth birthday, he'd taken the only family photo he owned out of his desk. It was a simple picture of him standing between his parents at a carnival, a reminder that things hadn't always been so dire. Authorities found it on the highest peak of the potato shrine, the sharp edge of the stalk impaling Tucker's childish face.

The first victim was a tourist who had the unfortunate luck of hiking through one of three trails in Marlowe. Tucker was on his way out. He'd packed lightly, taking his laptop and camera.

Tucker heard the hiker long before they met face to face. He recalled her being very pretty in a celebrity sort of way: long blond hair, tied back into a ponytail, flawless skin that shimmered with sweat, and a body that would've driven the average male to the point of lust. But Tucker was not the average male. Sexuality confused him. His hormones were conflicting. They drove him away from what would become his ultimate goal. He kept his urges in check and focused on the task at hand.

The woman, Celine Hawkins, did not see Tucker until he tripped her. She landed face down on the soil and woke several minutes later. Her shirt had been ripped off and her breasts were bare. Tucker had used the fabric to bind her hands and feet. He held the camera steady, a smile on his face. Reviewing the video, there is nothing sexual in the way he disrobed her. The frame does not linger on her anatomy. It stays close to her face, nearly unmoving, as he raises the large rock with his free hand and brings it down thirty-two times, eventually caving her skull. Dental records were needed to identify her body.

She screams once during the initial impact. Tucker later admitted he was disappointed in that first kill. He would learn to keep them alive longer, for the videos, for his growing fan base he did not yet know existed.

He traveled most of the next year, never settling in one spot for too long. Though he had no driver's license, he stole several vehicles with ease. He'd learned from simple instructions online. The Internet, he stressed time and time again, was the source of all the world's knowledge. Much like the dark, it could change you if you allowed it.

He picked up odd jobs, all of them under the table for obvious reasons. During a stint as a landscaper for a theme park mogul, while staying at a one-star motel, Tucker decided to upload that first video of the hiker. He wanted her death to mean something. He wanted, unsurprisingly, to gain recognition for what he'd done.

It was too risky to use a popular video sharing website. Such violence would be taken down quickly, especially if it was deemed to be real. He was familiar with the dark web, had traveled its digital pathways on more than one occasion, but so did the CIA and FBI. The majority of activities taking place in the underbelly of cyberspace were of the illegal variety. It was too risky, especially if he planned on more killing. Which he did.

He decided to upload the video to a forum. He searched for websites dedicated to snuff films. Most of the users, much like police officials, debated their existence to begin with. Tucker thought it was a good place to start. He could pretend the video was fiction, just a student film with realistic special effects. He chose a nondescript title (*Girl gets head bashed in*) and pressed enter. He felt a moment's hesitation, wondering if he ought to cancel. Not because of guilt or shame, but because he did not want to be caught so early in his quest.

But all those hours alone had worked to his advantage. He could evade being caught if need be. Tucker had developed computer skills that rivaled those of a professional hacker. In fact, several such individuals were recruited after his videos became more widespread. It took a team of nearly thirty to finally track him down. By then, of course, it was much too late.

Tucker watched the screen, refreshing every few moments, hoping someone had finally noticed him—or at least his work. He was in luck. The first response was simple, a bit obvious for his taste, but he smiled nonetheless.

Comment one: *That shit is sick.*

Thanks, Tucker typed.

Comment two: *For real. How you do that?*

Trade secret ;)

Comment three: *The way she screams and twitches, you'd think it ain't even fake.*

That's because it isn't.

Comment four: *Ha, ha, I bet. What're you a cereal killer or sumthin?*

Not yet. You need to kill three or more people. This is my first.

Comment five: *LOL, you crazy. You got anymore?*

No. Would you watch if I did?

Comment six: *Hell yeah. I'd watch the shit out of those.*

Your wish is my command :)

By the end of the night, there were over one hundred comments, with triple the amount of views. Two days later, it reached the thousands and grew from there. Tucker, for the first time in his life, was no longer alone. Even if he hadn't met them face-to-face, these forum users appreciated what he'd done. So what if they thought it was just movie magic? They'd know the truth soon enough when more videos appeared.

A star was born.

Tucker Ashton killed a total of twenty-seven people during his travels from the east coast to the west. As of this writing, there are four other murders reported to be connected to his trip but are yet unproven. The same is true of more than a dozen disappearances in the Midwest. Many of Tucker's videos were eventually taken down by fellow hackers and supporters only to be uploaded on, ironically, the dark web.

Perhaps his most infamous victim before traveling back to Marlowe was Scott Baker. Police tried to connect him to Tucker, to pinpoint a pattern or clue from his death. It was, after all, the only message Tucker had left the world.

I'll be seeing you.

That's what was written with Scott's blood in the bathroom of the one-bedroom apartment he shared with his girlfriend, Ivy Longwood. The couple had been together for just one year, had met at their day job, teaching at a private school in Oregon. Due to a rather rigid nepotism policy, either he or she would need to find work elsewhere, lest they both be terminated. Scott volunteered once their relationship was made public, though Ivy protested. She was a new hire, had less tenure, but Scott insisted. He would find a new job so they could be together without hesitation. Friends and relatives recall their romance with smiling faces. It was, by all accounts, true love.

Days before Scott had an interview at a school twenty miles south of their apartment, he was eviscerated in his bathroom tub. Ivy was the one to find him. She called the cops immediately, claiming at the time that she thought she heard someone else in the apartment, footsteps in her bedroom. She waited outside for the police and was certain no one exited. The back door had been boarded up while the fire escape was being worked on. There was only one way in and out. Tucker Ashton had not been spotted doing either. The murder was not connected to him until the video surfaced several days later.

Authorities questioned Ivy over the next weeks and months, attempting to decipher the message. Had she ever come in contact with Tucker? Was she aware of his videos? Had she ever downloaded any of them? Did Scott give any indication he'd met Ashton or commented on any of his websites? The answer to each of these questions was a resounding *no*, which makes Tucker's only written message all the more puzzling to this day.

I'll be seeing you.

But where?

TWELVE

MARIAH LONGWOOD GROANED. "What do you mean she's not missing?"

The voice on the other end of the phone sounded comatose. She imagined the woman as fat as could be, feet up on her desk and attempting a crossword puzzle. "I'm sorry, ma'am, but a person can't be considered missing unless twenty-four hours have passed. And you said it's been, what, less than twelve?"

She tried to do the math but her mind spun in every direction. "I guess about that. But like I told you, she went to Marlowe, Massachusetts."

"What's your point, ma'am?"

"My *point* is her boyfriend was murdered by the sicko that *came* from there. The same sicko that went back there and killed hundreds of people."

"You mean Tucker Ashton."

Mariah rolled her eyes. "Yes, that's exactly who I mean."

"But he's dead."

She pressed the crown of her nose and bit her lip against the oncoming migraine. She could feel it behind her eyes, shooting white-hot pain into her temples. She'd been having them more and more lately, as Ivy's symptoms worsened. And now that she was missing, the pain would not let up. It stayed with her everywhere she went. It was, she supposed, a lot like her sister's invisible blood.

"Are you still there? I said he's dead."

"I heard you the first time but *who* says he's dead? It's not confirmed. In fact, why does everyone insist he's dead at all? He disappeared. They never found a body. Just because he hasn't killed in a while doesn't mean he won't start up again."

A pause on the other line. She could practically see the woman holding in a laugh, pressing a flabby hand to her flabby stomach to keep the giggle at bay. "Look, I'm sorry about your sister. I know this is stressful but she's probably just avoiding you. That's what sisters do, right? If she's still missing tomorrow night, we'll put out an alert. Until then, there's nothing we can do."

Mariah gritted her teeth. The headache worsened. She imagined it materializing into something tall and skeletal, something Tucker Ashton-like that grabbed the nearest chef's knife and stabbed it into her skull. At least then, maybe some of the pressure would be released.

The woman cleared her throat. For a moment, Mariah had forgotten she was still on the phone. "Is there anything else I can help you with today?"

"No. As a matter of fact, you haven't been the least bit helpful. Have a great fucking day." She ended the call and checked for missed texts or messages. There was nothing. She reviewed her last twenty texts to her sister, all of them desperate. The same went for her calls, which went straight to Ivy's voicemail.

Mariah had warned her about that place. She knew it wasn't haunted. It was nothing so simple as ghosts or ghouls that threatened her sister. The reality was far more complicated and troublesome. Because killers *did* exist. As did depression. As did the word that kept swimming through Mariah's mind, floating to the surface of her migraine every so often just to remind her of its presence.

Suicide.

She hadn't thought Ivy capable of such a thing. Not even after Scott ...

She shook her head and recalled the days following his murder, how Ivy grew catatonic, staring at walls for hours. Only eating when food was forced in front of her. Drinking nothing but coffee and not bothering to hide her smoking. Mariah begged her to cry, let loose, scream at the sky if need be. Her sister had remained a statue through it all, holding back all emotions until one day, Mariah assumed, they would get the best of her.

What if they finally did *get the best of her? What if she checked into Hotel Marlowe, downed a bottle of sleeping pills, and went to bed forever?*

She shook away the thought. She was almost certain it wasn't the case.

Almost being the key word.

For the rest of the afternoon she kept busy with chores. She swept the floors despite them being clean enough to lick. She sprayed and wiped every window in the house. She searched for invisible dust bunnies. Mariah was pushing thirty-five, had no romance in her life unless you counted the occasional one-night stand, always at the man's house and never here with Ivy one room away. Though she wanted to get married, the right guy hadn't come along and it was looking more and more likely the right guy didn't exist.

Though she'd never admit it aloud, she'd been *jealous* of her sister and Scott. What they had—it was the stuff of romantic comedies. There didn't seem to be any issues between the two. She wanted that. Someone to hold and kiss and laugh. Someone to help push back the loneliness.

Which is why she'd been more affected than she cared to admit by Scott's death. On account of the half dozen times they'd slept together.

Which is why, even after two years had passed, despite her sister's troubling behavior, she still resented Ivy. In some weird way, she even *blamed* her.

She'd never told Ivy about her and Scott's time together. It had happened early on in their relationship. They'd been seeing each other for only a few weeks. Scott was due at Ivy's old apartment but it was Mariah who opened the door and welcomed him in, told him Ivy would be right out of the shower.

Over the next several weeks they spent precisely six sweaty nights panting in a motel until he broke it off. They made a promise never to speak of their act aloud.

There you had it. Even when everything seemed perfect on the surface, there was always something close by to ruin the façade.

In this case, it hadn't even been the infidelity.

It had been a madman with a knife and a fan base.

She moved onto Ivy's room, the messiest of the house. Here, the dust was visible. It covered everything. She swept and mopped and gagged when she spotted the sheets. They were yellowed and hardened with some mystery stain. The closer she got, the more she suspected it was sweat, as if they hadn't been washed since ...

Since Scott.

She stripped the bed and dragged the sheets across the hall, tossed them into the washing machine. As she made to turn it on, her headache protested. The pain grew exponentially. She slid to the floor and cried for a long time. She wiped her nose, rubbed her temples, and came to a conclusion.

Ivy had run into trouble, whatever that might mean, and Mariah didn't intend on sitting back. Not with equal doses of worry and guilt weighing her down, pushing her mind to the point of no return.

If the cops wouldn't help, Mariah would.

THIRTEEN

"SMOKE?" IVY HANDED Ethan a pack of Marlboros that had been full thirty minutes prior. Now it was more than half empty.

He shook his head. "No, thanks. I quit last year."

She nodded, stared through the windshield at the impossible crack in the ground. "Me too."

They hadn't spoken much since learning they wouldn't be leaving Marlowe tonight. On account of there being no way out. The old man from earlier, the one from the convenience store, had stared in their direction. He *had* to have seen them. Except he hadn't.

Which meant one of two things.

Either the three individuals sitting in the idling PT Cruiser had lost their minds or everything was real. Ethan begged for the first theory to be true but his gut told him otherwise. "We need food."

Ivy inhaled, held the smoke, exhaled. He coughed but she didn't offer to roll down the window. He didn't blame her. It felt almost safe inside the car. "Eating isn't exactly my top priority right now."

"I understand but when was the last time you ate *anything*? We're running on booze and adrenaline. Both will start to wear off soon."

"What did you have in mind? Is there a four-star restaurant in town? Maybe we could share some steaks with a serial killer and his biggest fan."

He winced. Hearing it spoken aloud was enough to bring his nerves back to life. Enough to remind him the second theory truly was the right one. "There's a diner back the way we came. We don't even have to take Main Street. I know a shortcut."

"How convenient." More smoke, less emotion. There'd been a change in her over the short time they'd known each other. She'd hardened up, perhaps her way of coping with the nightmare they'd been thrust into.

Thrust? You came here willingly, didn't you?

But that wasn't exactly the truth. He'd robbed a pharmacy willingly but he'd planned on dropping the pills off in Revere, not Marlowe. He'd been tricked by forces that were very much out of his control. He was called back here, whether by Tucker or something else. He thought of the bag of stolen meds, still sitting in his hotel room. Were they in the same spot on the floor or had something moved them? And if so, what did that something look like? Was it tall and frail or short and shriveled? Was it Tucker or something worse?

Nothing is worse.

He scanned the dark trees, sensing that *something* scanned back. "We should go. Once we're thinking straight, we can come up with a plan."

Ivy studied the road. He wondered if she saw something he didn't. "You direct. Once we're there, once we've filled our little bellies, no more lying. Deal?"

"What do you mean?"

"You can cut the bullshit. I have a feeling there wasn't trash in that bag. I believe you're from here, that you knew *him*, but there's something you're not telling me."

"Fair enough. But that goes for you too. I want to know why the hell you'd come to this place."

She tossed her butt out the window, the ember glowing in the thick darkness. "Sure. I've got to warn you, though. It's going to sound crazy."

"Try me."

Ivy swerved to miss a pothole. "Your streets suck here."

"They used to be better." Ethan thought back to when Marlowe wasn't such a bad place, when it had been somewhat of a home. It was hard to remember such days.

"I thought you said this place was nearby?"

"It's only another minute or so. It would've been quicker through downtown but I don't like the idea of passing the hotel again." He pointed to River Road. "Turn here and follow the water."

The road was covered in shadows, the headlights not offering much illumination. The darkness was solid somehow, more like sludge than air. On the left he spotted the river. It was dark but he swore the water looked unnatural, red like blood. It could've been his nerves but it was probably closer to the truth.

He looked into the sky again and was not surprised to find it void of any light. He cleared his throat, tried to sound less scared than he felt. "There aren't any stars."

"What?"

"In the sky, I mean. Did you notice that? It's just … pure blackness."

She looked through the window, nodded slowly. "I guess you're right. Doesn't seem possible, does it?"

"Nothing about this place is possible." He turned his head back to the road and grabbed the wheel when he saw the object blocking the way. "Watch out!"

She followed his line of sight and slammed onto the brakes. For the second time that night, they narrowly avoided a collision. She tried to catch her breath and pointed. "What the hell is that thing?"

"It's my car."

"What?"

He stepped out of the Cruiser without answering, walked toward the ruined vehicle he'd slid into the river earlier. Now it was back in the road and looked as if it had aged a hundred years. The metal was rusted and crushed beyond repair. Some of the dents resembled teeth marks. Every window had been shattered, the upholstery shredded.

"What the hell happened to it?" Ivy said from behind.

"I tossed it into the water earlier."

"So no one would find it." It wasn't a question. "Does this have something to do with your mystery bag?"

He nodded, tried to tell himself it wasn't the same car, but as he stepped closer he was certain of two things.

One: it *was* the same car. The vanity license plate remained unharmed, the Red Sox logo looking almost new.

Two: those *were* teeth marks and those *were* claw marks and they *were* being watched this very moment.

"We have to go," he said, backing away. The leaves to their right rustled. Something was close by. He smelled rotten garbage and something vaguely sweet, the scent of things left to rot. "You think you can get around it?"

"It'll be a tight fit. You want to tell me what's going on?"

"Not until this thing is in the rearview."

They sped into the Cruiser, locked the doors. Ivy turned the wheel.

From the backseat, something moved. Ethan was certain it was the thing hiding behind the trees, the thing that smelled so horrid. A moment later, Amy yawned and stretched and asked where they were going.

"To eat something and get the hell out of this place." Ivy pulled onto the shoulder. She'd been right. It was tight but they managed to pass the wreck. The leaves and trees swayed violently as if pushed by a gust of wind that wasn't there.

As if the thing moving the trees was frustrated.

As the Cruiser turned the corner, he spotted something as it stepped onto the road. Something tall and misshapen. Then it was gone, swallowed by the darkness, though it didn't feel far away.

In Marlowe, the bad things were never far away.

FOURTEEN

"IT'S JUST UP here," Ethan said a few minutes later.

Ivy slowed the car. The country road became a bit less rural. There were businesses every few blocks but they'd long since closed their doors. Most of the windows had been boarded up, blocking any view of the interior. The signs and slogans had faded with time. She wondered what they could've been. Hardware stores perhaps. Maybe video rental shops that had closed when Blockbuster reigned. Were the video tapes still inside, gathering dust, or had the display room been cleared out, leaving behind only bare walls?

She was beginning to suspect the latter was true, that everything in this town had gone out of business. "Are you sure about this?"

He pointed. "Turn here."

She pulled into a gravel parking lot. The wheels spun, pebbles shooting in every direction. She imagined the car sinking until they were submerged. Suffocation, she reasoned, was preferable to what she'd already seen tonight.

The Marlowe Diner, much like every other establishment in town, had seen better days. It resembled a train cart, its shape reminiscent of other such restaurants, but that's where the resemblance ended. The metal siding was badly dented, not unlike the wreckage back on River Road. The windows weren't boarded up but they were yellowed beyond return. It made everything on the other side look distorted. She squinted and told herself nothing moved among the booths and bar.

She parked and cut the engine. "Let's make it quick."

"No," Amy said from the backseat. "No, no, no. We need to get out of here now."

"We will," Ethan said as he stepped out. "But we can't do anything until we've eaten. Until we've come up with a plan."

Amy crossed her arms and pouted, child-like. It was, Ivy supposed, something she did often back home. Zeke had probably spoiled her, and in return, she'd given him her undying allegiance. That is, until he'd brought her to a town where bartenders walked around with axes sticking from their spines. Which reminded her. "We need a weapon. Something to defend ourselves with in case we're not the only ones dining tonight."

Ethan waved his hands. "I've got nothing. We can grab a knife inside. Maybe some pans too."

She eyed him, tried to tell if he was lying. "You sure you don't have a gun on you?"

"You want to search me?" He turned around and headed for the entrance.

Ivy waved Amy on. "Stay out here if you want but I wouldn't. There's safety in numbers and tonight, we seem to be the only three people with our heads still attached to our shoulders. So to speak."

Amy got the message. She nearly tripped on her way out of the car.

Ethan reached the door. Ivy expected him to break the glass but instead he turned the knob and it opened with ease. He held it while they entered.

The diner smelled halfway between mold and sweat, a pile of dirty laundry left out for ages. There were a dozen booths and a rectangular bar faced an open kitchen. She could see knives on the closest counter. "Grab one of those," she said.

Ethan nodded and stepped into the kitchen.

She led Amy to the closest booth but didn't sit down. "Where are you going?" the girl asked.

Ivy didn't answer. She stepped behind the bar, stood on the counter, and leaned into the kitchen. After a few moments of searching, she settled on a large ice pick. It wasn't the world's thickest piece of metal but it would do the trick. She slid it into the handles of the front door and tested them. It held but it wouldn't hold up against something larger than human.

She sat across from Amy. The two did not speak for a long time. It wasn't an awkward silence. They'd shared near-death experiences. They were more than strangers now, shared a common bond most others didn't.

The smell of something cooking drifted in from the kitchen. The griddle sizzled and she thought she heard a microwave. Her mouth watered. Ethan had been right. Fear caused quite the famish.

Five minutes passed. The kitchen door opened and Ethan carried three plates toward their booth. He set them down and apologized. "This was the best I could do. Almost everything's gone bad."

Ivy looked at her plate. It wasn't exactly gourmet but it called to her nonetheless. A pile of corned beef hash, with a side of mixed vegetables.

Amy shook her head, looked ready to cry.

"What's the matter?" Ethan said.

"I'm a vegetarian."

He lifted his plate. "Here, have my vegetables." He exchanged them for her helping of hash and sat down.

After shoving several forkfuls into his mouth, he reached for the floor. "There's something wrong with this place. Aside from the obvious, I mean." He lifted a bag of bread and set it on the table. Ivy nearly choked when she saw the dark blue tint of the dough, how it had turned to mold so badly it looked malignant.

"Jesus, how old is that thing?"

He pointed to the sticker. "That's what I'm getting at. Look."

The expiration date hadn't yet passed. Four days remained.

"How is that possible?" Amy said, looking away as she ate her vegetables and plugged her nostrils.

"I'm not sure," Ethan said. "But I'm open to theories."

Ivy forced down a bite of hash. It was salty and sour but it filled the pang in her belly somewhat. "There'll be plenty of time for theories and plans but first things first. What was in the bag?"

"Are you thirsty? I'm thirsty. I'll grab us some water."

Before she could protest he was up and walking into the kitchen, taking his time with their beverages. He walked slowly back toward the table, his head down. He would not meet either of their eyes, either embarrassed or ashamed or both.

She sipped her water, gave him a moment to begin. It tasted stale, faintly metallic, but she chugged it nonetheless.

"Pills," he finally said. Instead of sitting back down, he began to pace. "The bag was filled with pills."

She nodded for him to go on.

"The kind that are only legal if prescribed by a medical professional. The kind that are in high demand with the junkie crowd." He shook his head. "The kind someone desperate might be convinced into stealing for the right price."

"Care to tell us who that someone is?" Ivy said.

"It wasn't my fault. Not really, at least. My brother, Andrew, convinced me. That prick. He's only been out of jail for a few months. I'll give you three guesses what he was in for."

"Come from a family of thieves, do you?"

He laughed. There was nothing funny about the gesture. "No, it's not like that. I'm a loan officer. I wear a tie and sit at a desk all day. I work at a gas station by night."

"Don't loan officers make good money?" This from Amy. She'd finished her vegetables and eyed Ethan's hash as if she might switch teams before the night ended.

"Sure," he said. "But my kitchen table is piled high with medical bills. Every time I walk by, one of them lands at my feet. How's that for symbolism?"

"What's wrong with you?" Ivy said.

He scratched at his stubble, nails on a chalkboard in the silence of the diner. "Not me. It's my daughter, Lisa. She has ..." He trailed off, wiped his eyes. "She has cancer. God, I hate that fucking word. She has cancer and she's fighting it tooth and nail, and she's doing well—great even. The doctors expect a full recovery. But no amount of medical insurance covers something like that. It's like buying a car every time they put a needle in her arm. So even with two jobs, it wasn't enough. Andrew got me drunk, played on my fears, tricked me into stealing a bag of pills from a pharmacy."

"Why Marlowe, though?" Ivy said.

"Here's where it gets crazy. The paper he gave me with the buyer's address? It said Hotel Marlowe. At least the first dozen times I read it. But when I checked the thing again at the hotel, it had changed."

"Changed?"

He nodded, paced, nodded, paced. "Like this place was tricking me. Like *Tucker* was tricking me."

They grew quiet. Ivy didn't like that last implication. Not because she thought it was crazy—of course it was crazy—but because it seemed like the most plausible theory.

Ethan refilled her glass, set it back down on the table. "Your turn."

She nodded, lit another cigarette. With the windows closed, the smoke gathered quickly. "I guess I was tricked too. Not into robbing. Nothing so simple as that. See, that bastard killed my boyfriend." She held up her ring. "You asked me if I was married earlier? Well, I'm not. I found this in his bureau after the police peeled his body out of a bathtub. As far as I can tell, Scott was going to propose that weekend. I had the distinct honor of being widowed by Tucker Ashton. Scott was his last victim before he came back and slaughtered half the town."

Ethan ran a hand through his greasy hair. "Jesus."

"It gets worse. I didn't come here on a whim. I came here because Tucker left behind a cute little message in my boyfriend's blood. He wrote me a note on the bathroom wall. It said 'I'll be seeing you.'" She held in the smoke, wondered how long she could keep it up before she finally coughed it out. "Here's where you think *I'm* crazy."

"No one thinks you're crazy," Amy said. She'd caved and scooped a healthy portion of Ethan's hash on her plate. He didn't seem to notice.

"I wasn't going to come here," Ivy said. "But a few months ago, I started seeing blood. I don't mean I cut my finger or anything like that. I mean I saw blood that wasn't there. Not that anyone else could see, at least. But let me assure you, it was there for me. In my bed and in my car and at my work. Even when I closed my eyes. My shrink said it was normal. That sound normal to you?"

Her question went unanswered.

She tapped ashes onto her plate. "I got to thinking. Maybe I was being called here for some reason. I didn't expect to meet the maniac that did it. I just thought, maybe if I came here and faced my demons ..." She winced at the terminology. "Maybe I'd find closure. I see now I was wrong."

They both turned to Amy.

Ivy cleared her throat. "And then there was one."

Amy looked up and shrugged. "What do you want to know?" In the dim light she looked no older than sixteen.

"The same thing we just said for ourselves," Ethan answered. "Why Marlowe?"

She stopped eating, stared at something far in the distance. Something neither Ethan nor Ivy could see. "I don't have anything special to tell you. I wasn't called here by mysterious circumstances. Tucker didn't kill anyone I know. Not literally at least."

"How do you mean?" Ethan eyed Ivy's cigarette. She could feel him itching for a smoke. Once you started, it was always with you. Just because you quit didn't mean you weren't an addict.

"Tucker killed Zeke in a way. Zeke was already obsessed by the time we started dating. It started when he was younger. But it was harmless, you know? Sure, he ran a website dedicated to killers but he wasn't hurting anyone. He wasn't a killer himself. But one night, he started sleepwalking, started writing letters to himself like they were from Tucker. I didn't have the heart to tell him otherwise. It sounds sick, but Tucker was—*is*—his hero. I figured there was no sense in spoiling the illusion. He thought it was a good idea to come to Marlowe. Read it in one of his sleep letters. And here we are."

"It sounds like you didn't want to come here so why give in?" Ethan said.

She blinked away tears but they were instantly replaced. "Because he's the only person left in my life. It's a long story. I know he's not the world's greatest boyfriend but he takes care of me. He makes me feel like I'm needed. If it weren't for him, if he was gone ..." She wiped her nose with a crumpled napkin. "I guess he *is* gone. That wasn't the same man I knew tonight, in that room with Tucker. In that *television* studio."

Ivy had nearly forgotten about that part. Fear and exhaustion played with your head. "Which brings us to the million-dollar question."

Amy sniffled. "You mean why there's a giant crack in the ground?"

"I mean what the fuck is wrong with Marlowe, Massachusetts?"

Ethan opened his mouth to respond but his words were cut off and his eyes were drawn elsewhere. Ivy followed them, saw the object hurling toward the nearest window just before it crashed through. Broken shards littered their table.

Something landed on the table in front of them.

FIFTEEN

A KNOCK AT the door.

Brad Ashton ignored it. He faced the only window in the microscopic room. It was almost light outside, the darkness fading. The horizon was pink, the clouds like cotton candy, and he took solace in this. He found himself doing that more often these days. Recognizing the beauty in simple things, things he never used to notice.

Probably, he thought, because time was ticking and he didn't have that many sunrises left to witness.

Another knock. "Mr. Ashton? You have a visitor."

He groaned. "Do you know what time it is?"

The nurse—it sounded like Sophia but could've been Andrea—opened the door a crack. "It sounds urgent."

He could've laughed at that. He couldn't remember the last time someone had come to see him. There was no one left to bring urgent news. He was an old and bitter man and would almost certainly die alone.

An estranged friend then. Someone who'd lost touch and tracked him down. Someone who hadn't given up on Brad entirely. It seemed unlikely but it was the only theory he had. "Send them in then."

The nurse—Sophia after all—poked her head into his room and nodded.

The door opened, revealing a man Brad had never met. A stranger who somehow seemed familiar. He didn't believe in déjà vu but he *did* believe in trusting your gut. And right now his gut was sending out warnings left and right.

The man smiled. Brad's stomach revolted. He thought he'd lose what little he'd eaten in the last twenty-four hours. No, not eaten. Drank was more like it. That had been the worst part about the stroke. He could take the numbness, the occasional fatigue—hell, even the speech impediment—but he would never adjust to drinking a Salisbury steak through a straw.

The man whispered something into Sophia's ear—a joke, judging by her laughter. She slapped him on the shoulder. It was playful, flirtatious, and it reminded Brad of better days. Days when he could still get a hard on, when it was fathomable that a woman would take him to bed.

Days when his wife was alive, before he'd become the son of a bitch he was now.

Sophia told the man she'd be back in fifteen minutes. Breakfast was coming. Another liquefied concoction to slurp through his partially paralyzed mouth.

The man winked at her. "We'll be quick." He turned to Brad. "I promise."

The door closed. It was perhaps the loudest sound Brad Ashton ever heard. A gunshot in the early morning calm.

"Who the hell are you?" Though it came out jumbled, Brad got his point across.

"I'm a friend of the family."

"The hell you are. I've never seen you before. And besides, I ain't got a family."

The man walked toward the window, gazed outside. The pink had come closer. "Beautiful, isn't it?"

Brad shrugged. "It's something to look at. What did you say your name was again?"

"I didn't." The man pulled from his pocket a folded piece of paper. He unwrinkled it and read whatever was written, mumbling to himself. It was the face of someone studying before an exam. "He says you've been expecting this."

"Expecting what exactly? And who said that?"

That smile again. Brad's skin shriveled in response, the wrinkles growing even deeper for a moment. "Who do you think?"

"Look, what's this about? I'm tired and hungry. It's going to be a long day and I'd rather not spend it with someone who's out of their mind."

The man nodded. "He said you'd say that too."

"Who said—"

"Your son, Mr. Ashton. Your son sent me."

The silence that followed was thick. It floated about the room, like the morning clouds had forced themselves through the glass. Only these were storm clouds, no longer pink and dream-like. They were black as night and they brought thunder with them. "My son, you said?"

"Tucker asked that I get you. He said it's very important you come with me."

"Why would I do that? My son is dead."

The man laughed. "Don't tell me you believe that. I expected more from you. You must have felt it in your bones. Mr. Ashton, you would know if your son was dead. I promise you he's not."

Brad eyed the button near his bed, the one he refused to use even when he needed help. He was an adult, not an infant, though the staff at Meadow Farms Nursing Facility, located just twenty miles south of Marlowe, seemed to forget that. Now it called to him like a beacon of hope. It was miles away, especially with the wheelchair.

The man caught him staring. He tsk-tsked and tossed the button across the bed. It landed on the floor with a thud. He sat down on the comforter and winced. "You actually sleep in this thing?"

"I'd like you to leave now. Or I'll call for help."

"Try it. I'd love to see you open that mouth of yours and actually get a scream out. No one's going to hear you, Brad."

He noted the change from his last to first name. Less formal. This part, more than anything in the last few minutes, scared Brad. "I don't want trouble. Just leave me be."

"The problem is trouble *found you*. You wanted to know my name. It's Zeke. I'm a fan of your son's work, have been for a long time. You may have thought he was a sicko but to me—hell, to *all* his fans—he's more than that. He's a role model."

"A role model? My son needed help. *Psychiatric* help. I should've sent him away before it was too late."

"You made your son into a monster, Brad. Whether or not you want to believe that. What he became, all those people he killed—that was mostly your doing. You can either feel guilty or proud but you've got to feel something. You can't sit around here, pissing your pants and pretending the past didn't happen. That's why Tucker sent me. We're going to have a family reunion."

The thought of his son, all grown up, living and breathing after killing so many people, gave his heart a boost of adrenaline. He tensed, made to roll out of his chair, but the man—Zeke—was already standing and holding him back. "Tucker said you were a stubborn bastard. He wasn't kidding."

Brad stared him in the eyes. They were vacant, the pupils dilated beyond return. They were, he realized, exactly how his son's had been. Too similar to be a coincidence.

This freak has my son's eyes.

Before he could make sense of this revelation, Zeke pulled from his pocket what looked like a syringe. "Your son is a genius, you know. Not only is he a talented killer but he has a way with knowing things a normal person couldn't. Like exactly where the sedatives are stored in this place." He popped the cap off, flicked the needle so the air bubbles escaped. "This will only hurt for a moment."

He stabbed it into Brad's arm. It took effect quickly. His body grew tired. His muscles relaxed against his will. His eyelids tripled their weight.

"Don't fight," Zeke said. "Just go to sleep. When you wake up, you'll be back in your old home, back in Marlowe, with your son. He'll be so happy to see you."

SIXTEEN

"YOU'RE BLEEDING," ETHAN said. "Both of you."

Ivy looked at her arm. There was a small incision, leaking freely. She grabbed a napkin and held it against the wound. Her face contorted with pain but it was a superficial wound.

They both turned to Amy. She hadn't been so lucky. Her mouth was open in shock. A shard of glass stuck out of her leg, just above the knee. Ethan wondered how deep it went.

"Can you walk?" Ivy reached over the table and helped her up from the mess.

Amy shook her head. "I don't think so." She tried standing but her scream was answer enough. They carried her over to the bar, leaned her against the metal.

"We've got to clean it," Ivy said. She didn't sound as calm anymore. Whatever change had taken place since they saw the crack in the earth, whatever bravery she'd gained from all this, was slowly fading.

Ethan sped into the kitchen, came back with a glass of water and a dirty rag.

"Are those clean?" Amy said between hyperventilating.

"Probably not." Ethan handed the rag to Ivy. "But it's the best we've got." He poured the water over the wound. "We've got to get the glass out."

Amy shook her head. "No way. Don't they say to keep it in? Don't they say that makes it worse?"

"He's right," Ivy said. "It could get infected." Without waiting for a response, she tied the rag around Amy's thigh and tightened it. "This might hurt a bit." She pulled the glass out quickly.

Amy thrashed in place, nearly convulsing. Ethan cleaned the wound once more. The water turned red. He found another rag behind the bar, stiff with age, and tied it around the open wound as tight as he could manage.

It wasn't until they calmed Amy down some that Ethan remembered the object that had been hurled through the window. It lay on the table. He squinted, couldn't make it out from his location. For a moment, he thought it was a severed head. Perhaps Annabelle had followed them here. He rubbed his eyes. They must have been playing tricks. When he looked again he saw it was not a head but a large rock. A rock with a note attached by a rubber band.

He took his time walking toward the table. He did not want to read whatever was written on that piece of paper. If he avoided it, if his eyes never saw the message, then he'd be safe. He could figure out how to leave Marlowe and go back to his real life, no matter how stressful it had been. He knew it was a stupid theory, one his mind conjured as a coping mechanism, but it felt valid nonetheless.

He reached for the rock as he would a snake, holding his hand steady, certain it would uncoil and sink jagged fangs into the flesh of his palm. Sending poison into his blood stream, just like the cancer had done to Lisa.

When the rock did not bite, he uncoiled the rubber band and retrieved the note.

And wished upon all wishes he hadn't.

"What is it?" Amy and Ivy said in unison.

He didn't answer at first. He *couldn't*. Fear clenched his jaw, held it in place. Under other circumstances he would've thought the words were fake, that he'd lost his mind. But then he remembered where he was—where they all were—and he knew the words to be real. "It's an invitation."

"For what?" Their voices shook.

He cleared his throat. "Dear Ethan, Amy, and Ivy. You are cordially invited to the Ashton family reunion, taking place tonight at the Hotel Marlowe in lovely and historic Marlowe, Massachusetts. Enjoy unlimited cocktails and hors d'oeuvres, live music, and dancing. Fun will be had by all. No RSVP necessary. Attendance is mandatory." He paused, did not want to read on.

Amy whimpered. "Is that all?"

He shook his head. "There's more. But I don't think you want to hear it."

"You're probably right," Ivy said. "But read it anyway."

His throat was thick with bile and acid. "Please do not get any funny ideas like trying to leave. If you haven't noticed, there's no way out of Marlowe. This is my town now. My home. And if you ruin my party, you'll regret it. Hope to see you all there tonight. Yours truly. TA."

He crumpled the note but it didn't seem final enough. He walked back into the kitchen, lit the stove, and held the letter over the open flame, took great joy in watching it burn until only ash remained.

With the burner on, he gathered every last rag he could find and set them over the stove. They caught quickly, the age working in Ethan's favor. The flames grew. The kitchen filled with dark smoke. He coughed on his way out.

"Come on." He grabbed Amy's arm and steered her toward the entrance.

Ivy pulled the metal rod from the handles and opened the door. A chilly breeze blew from outside. It was disorienting. Frigid in the front, smoldering in the back. "Why'd you do that?" she said.

He shrugged, helped Amy down the stairs. "Because I wanted to. I want to burn every block of this town."

Ivy opened the back door of the PT Cruiser and Amy slid in. "Tell me we're not going to that party."

They sat down, slid on their seatbelts. Ethan started the engine, driving this time around. He clenched the steering wheel and looked into the rearview mirror. The diner was ablaze now. Several windows shattered from the heat. It felt good to watch the place turn to debris. He wondered if Tucker could see the smoke floating into the starless sky.

A hand on his arm. "Ethan?" Ivy said.

"Yeah?"

"The party. We're not going, right? We'd have to be crazy to go anywhere near that place."

"Of course not. But there's one problem we've overlooked all night."

"What's that?"

He put the car into drive. "This isn't the real Marlowe and we're sure as hell not in control."

He sped out of the parking lot, kicking up more rocks.

The diner continued to burn.

It came as no surprise the crack in the earth was farther spread than they'd hoped. It surrounded all of Marlowe, sealed it off from the rest of the real world. If you'd viewed the town from above, in a plane or helicopter, it would've looked perfectly symmetrical. A gouge in the planet's exterior that should not have been there.

Ethan steered the car around the town's perimeter, taking great care not to travel anywhere near its heart, near the hotel and the party.

In the backseat, Amy whimpered. It felt like that's all she'd done for the last twenty-four hours, perhaps longer. The pain in her leg grew worse with each movement. The rag was crimson now, not quite sopping with her blood but well on its way. It would not hold for long. If they didn't get her stitches in a functioning hospital … her mind trailed off. There was enough to worry about.

She heard Ethan and Ivy up front, cursing as they rode parallel to the crack, keeping their voices down so as not to scare the child in back. She didn't blame them. She was a weak, stupid girl who'd been drawn to Zeke like flies to shit. In a way, tonight was partly her fault. If she'd been able to convince Zeke to call the trip off, if she'd confronted him about his chosen line of work—

You think he would've listened? He would've come here with or without you. There's nothing you could've done. You're nothing more than a set of tits and a pussy to him.

She shook her head. That wasn't true. Not exactly. Zeke may not have been of the sanest mind during their relationship, but there *was* love there. Faint, sure. Buried under his website and his memorabilia and his sleep letters but present nonetheless.

Love or no love, look where it got you.

She forced back more tears coming. Her eyes were red and sore. She would not give her nerves the satisfaction of opening the floodgates again. She cursed the day she'd let life slip away from her.

She'd let her mother's death cripple her. She'd sat back and wallowed, cut everyone else out of her life. She could've used the death as a means to rekindle her relationship with her stepfather. She could've reached out to her old friends. Instead she'd grown lazy and lonely and now she sat in the backseat of a PT Cruiser with two strangers. In a foreign place that may not have existed to begin with.

She looked at the dashboard clock. It spun through numbers at random, never settling on any one digit. She looked at the black sky and noted another development.

"It should be morning by now."

Ethan and Ivy stopped discussing the crack. "How do you mean?" the latter said.

She nodded toward the sky. "I don't know what time we woke up at the hotel but it was hours ago. It should be morning, not night. Where the hell is the sun?"

Neither of them answered.

She tried to keep her panic at bay, to stop it from boiling up out of her chest. She could feel a scream forming in her throat. It was quite insistent on being let out.

"This isn't Marlowe," Ivy finally said. It did nothing for Amy's nerves but it delayed her inevitable breakdown for the moment.

"I beg to differ," Ethan said, his eyes following the crack.

"You grew up here," Ivy said to Ethan. "Does is it look like the same town you remember as a kid?"

"Of course not. That was twenty years ago. Times change and so do places."

Ivy lit another cigarette. The car filled with smoke, though no one dared to roll the windows down. "Tell me you don't feel it in the air. Tell me this place isn't haunted."

He scratched his face. The stubble had grown exponentially in the time Amy had known him. "Something is definitely wrong with Marlowe. There's no denying that. I didn't believe in ghosts this morning—or yesterday morning, whenever we got here—but now I'm not so sure."

Ivy nodded, blew smoke from her nostrils. "Then hear me out. This isn't the same Marlowe you remember. It isn't the *real* Marlowe. It's another version. We're not in control here. You said so yourself."

"Fair enough but if *we're* not ..." he trailed off.

"Tucker," Amy said, beating him to the punch. "Tucker is in

control, has been since we crossed the town line. Ivy's right. This isn't his real hometown. It's his own version of it."

"You're saying we came to a make-believe place created by a killer?" Ethan said.

Ivy snapped her fingers. "Bingo."

More silence. Heavy and thick like the darkness outside. They rode for what could've been hours. The landscape was all the same: trees and shadows and things that may or may not have hidden within them.

A question formed in Amy's mind. It was related to their new theory, only worse, like the answer was so above what her rational mind could handle, she'd crumble when she learned the truth. But her lips were already open and her jaw was already moving. "Why us?"

"I was going to ask the same thing," Ivy said. "In fact, that's all I've been able to think about tonight. We all have some connection to Tucker but so do hundreds of other people. Why choose three strangers?"

Ethan slowed the car. His eyes focused on something up ahead. "Impossible."

They looked through the windshield at the lights up ahead, the ones what were familiar by now. Amy was by no means an expert on Marlowe's landscape but she was certain they couldn't have traveled back to Main Street. Yet there it was, no more than a football field's distance away. Gone was the rural road they'd circled.

"It's the party," she said.

"What about it?" Ethan was already backing up, trying to get them away from the hotel. As if that were an option anymore.

Amy stared at the structures ahead, the shops and restaurants, the bar and hotel. "Attendance is mandatory, remember? We'll wind up back there whether or not we want to go."

"Not if I have any say in the matter," he said, speeding now.

They must have backed up a quarter of a mile by the time he spun the car in the opposite direction.

Yet the heart of Marlowe had only grown closer.

SEVENTEEN

BRAD ASHTON WOKE slowly, his lids sticking to his eyes. He made to move his hands but they didn't budge. His wrists were raw and numb at the same time. His feet followed suit, pins and needles crawling toward his knees. Darkness surrounded him, so thick it made no difference that his eyes were open.

For a moment he thought he'd fallen into a deep sleep. He did that often these days. The older he got, the stronger his dreams became.

And nightmares. He shivered just thinking about them. They'd grown worse over the last few years, ever since Tucker's rampage.

The thought of his son did something to his mind, unseen gears turning.

Ahead, in the sludge-like shadows, something skittered. It sounded close by, though he wasn't sure in which direction. The darkness played tricks with him but he was suddenly certain of one thing.

He was not alone.

He bit his lip, hoping to wake from the dream. He knew where this was heading. The same place they *always* headed. Diana would show up, bleeding out of the several stab wounds she'd suffered in reality. He'd been the one to identify her that night, after the mugging, after that sick fuck had taken her from him. The blood, he recalled, had still been seeping, even hours after the clotting began to take place. A punishment for becoming the man he had, for letting life turn him into a monster.

The old Brad—what little of him remained—died in that moment. Now there was only this husk, this decaying pile of skin and bones that would no doubt die in the next couple of years. Perhaps sooner if he didn't wake up.

He tasted something warm and coppery in his mouth. He'd been biting so hard he'd torn away a small bit of flesh. The taste seeped toward his throat. He swallowed.

You can't taste things in dreams.

There came more movement from nearby, another fluttering, skittering sound. His mind conjured a bird or bat but he knew it was nothing so innocent. He wasn't dreaming but wide awake and, if his memories of the man—had Zeke been his name?—were to be trusted, he knew exactly where he was.

A rectangle of light appeared up ahead. A figure stepped into the room. It seemed misshapen, walked with a horrid limp. Something stuck out of its back. He thought at first it was an extra limb, one arm or foot too many.

As his eyes adjusted he saw it was not a creature but a man, though that did not help his hammering heart. An axe hung out of the stranger's back. The wound had grown infected, as had the rest of his body. His skin was gray with death, not unlike Diana's had been that night.

He squinted and realized he was not just a stranger.

"I was starting to think you'd never wake up," Jacob said. Most of his teeth were gone. Those that remained had rotted. A flurry of flies hung above him. That accounted for the sound.

"I'd be so lucky," Brad said, spitting a wad of blood onto the floor.

"Knock it off with that, will you? I just cleaned this place up for the party."

"Party?"

Jacob nodded. "Your boy's gone through a lot of trouble to make this night special. If I were you, I'd make an effort to seem appreciative. Hell, if you play your cards right, maybe he'll even let you live." A fly landed on his wound, dining on the blackened flesh. He didn't seem to notice.

"You're not real," Brad said.

"You're talking to me, aren't you?"

"You've been dead for two years."

"Going on three actually." He scratched at a scab on his shoulder blade. A chunk of skin fell to the floor. Brad swore he saw it slither away of its own accord.

"Then how the hell are you standing there with an axe in your back instead of in a casket? I went to your funeral."

"How was it?"

Brad bowed his head, willed himself to go back to sleep. The coma-like blackness had been much better than this. "You want to tell me what the hell's going on?"

"It would take hours. We don't have that kind of time. I'll give you an abbreviated version. You deserve that much. You were one of my biggest customers after all. You put my kids through college."

"Don't mention it."

Jacob extended his fingers. Several flies landed in the palm of his hand. He petted them like puppies. "You ever heard of mind over matter?"

"I guess so."

"There's documented proof of that sort of thing, people bending spoons with their mind, moving objects just by concentrating. This place is no different. Tucker—he wanted a town of his own, one where he was in control. He wanted to be the ruler, the mayor, the king. You catch my drift?"

Brad shook his head but Jacob went on.

"And when you want something bad enough, when you concentrate all your energy and willpower on one thing, sometimes it happens, you know?"

No, I don't know. I've wanted to have my wife back for years now. I've thought about it every waking moment of my pathetic life. Yet she's still in the ground and I'm here in, what, a make believe town? A make believe Marlowe?

"Are you even listening?" Jacob said.

"I'm trying but it sounds a bit crazy."

He nodded. "I can see why you'd say that. Your son is a very special young man. He's capable of more than just killing. Tonight, you'll see the rest of his talents. Speaking of which …" He looked at his watch. The flies buzzed away from his fingers, forming a single organism above him, a black, swarming balloon. "It's almost party time." The watch was broken, a spider web of cracks. The minute and second hands, though—they moved quite freely, spinning in opposite direction like a compass in the Bermuda Triangle.

"You could let me go." Brad hated the sound of his voice, hated the way it begged and pleaded.

"No can do, boss." Jacob helped Brad to his feet, catching him when he nearly fell to the floor. "It's good to see you, though. You could be a real son of bitch but now and then, you were all right. Told a good joke, carried on a conversation with the best of them. When you had enough PBRs in you, that is." He pulled Brad out of the dark room and into the main area of Jacob's Pub. The place had seen better days. Floorboards were cracked. Tables were warped. The windows were yellowed and smudged but he could see Hotel Marlowe. Could see the movement over there, the shapes filing in the entrance excitedly.

He surrendered, allowed Jacob to guide him toward the exit and onto the street. His head hung low and he closed his eyes once again. "I just want to go home."

Jacob smiled, patted him on the back. "You are home, Brad."

"It's not working." Amy's voice went through phases of hysteria, screaming one moment, crying the next, then growing slow and steady as if she'd become catatonic.

Ivy didn't blame the girl one bit. Her own mind felt ready to come undone as she stared through the windshield toward the city center. Downtown was alive with movement, countless shapes walking and strolling and skipping toward the one place Ivy did not wish to see ever again. Every light in Hotel Marlowe glowed in the night.

The night that won't end, she thought. *I'll never see the sun again because the sun doesn't visit Marlowe. Not this Marlowe at least.*

"Faster," she told Ethan.

"I'm trying my best." His skin was soaked with sweat. His eyes had not blinked in the last ten minutes.

The faster they sped backward, the closer the town got. It was not possible yet it was the truth. Finally, he spun the Cruiser around and sped off in the opposite direction. The town, though it should have been behind them now, stood in their direct line of vision. It did not want them to leave. *Tucker* did not want them to leave.

The engine made a defeated noise, popping and crackling then hissing as the car died. The gas gauge was on empty. The lights turned off yet the radio turned on. Static filled the interior, piercing her ears. Odd circus music cut through the noise, distorted and sporadic, followed by a voice that sent her nerves into a frenzy.

"I see you got my invitation," Tucker said over the airwaves. "I'm so glad you could make it. As you may have noticed, this party has a way of … sucking people in. Try as you might, you're all residents of Marlowe now and we're so glad to have you."

Amy reached forward and pressed the power button. Tucker's voice did not stop. "As I was saying, it's nearly time for our big bash and you can't wander in wearing street clothes. It's high time you freshened up."

"What the hell's he talking about?" Ethan said.

Before Ivy could respond, they got their answer in the form of several shapes stepping out of the darkness. The doors opened with such force the metal tore from its hinges. The shapes tossed the doors onto the ground and ripped through their seatbelts with ease. The one that grabbed Ivy was obese beyond return, bloated even worse by death. The man's skin was the color of ash. His jaw was missing. In its place, a loose tongue slithered, worm-like, trying to find its missing companion.

On the other side of the Cruiser, Ethan fell to the ground. A woman stood above him. She was old, her hair the same color as her dead skin. One of her eyes was bruised shut. The other one hung loose by its optical nerve, swinging every so often like a pendulum. It was soothing in a sick sort of way. Ivy felt her pulse slow as she was hauled away from the others. She did not struggle. Giving up felt much more apt.

Amy was pinned to the ground by what looked like a little girl. She couldn't have been older than ten, yet she held Amy in place without effort. The girl's lips were ruined, shredded so her teeth were visible even when she closed her mouth. She giggled as Amy struggled.

These were not just any dead people. They were Tucker's victims, those he'd slaughtered when he came back home. These were the same people she'd seen back at the hotel, clapping inside of the television studio that should not have existed. Jacob with his bloody axe. Annabelle with her severed head. All of them dead and resurrected at the hand of Tucker Ashton.

Ivy didn't have to ask where they were being taken. Not that the man without the jaw could've answered. Tucker wanted them scattered. There was strength in numbers. It was perhaps their only hope of escape. But now they were separated and that last bit of hope fled out of Ivy like a scab being torn away.

And scabs, Ivy knew, left quite nasty scars.

EIGHTEEN

MARIAH CALLED THE cops again. This time they listened. This time they put out an alert. Not that it would help. It had been a full two days and Ivy had ignored all of her texts and calls, the latter of which went straight to voicemail.

Before she'd made the decision to fly to Marlowe, Mariah had called the town's only hotel. She felt stupid for not thinking to do so earlier. She could at least verify Ivy had checked in. In fact, it was something the cops should have suggested to begin with. She thought again of the fat woman on the phone, smirking while she did her crossword, trying not to laugh as the crazy lady talked about Tucker Ashton.

She waited an eternity while the phone rang into her ear, yet no one picked up. She did some research, Googled the place, only to find it had no website. The more she looked into it, the more her desperation grew. Until she found her answer in an old newspaper article. The headline chilled her.

Hotel Marlowe Closes Its Doors.

It appeared the building had shut down not long after the massacre. There had been such a decline in tourism the owners couldn't sustain their business.

She shook her head, told herself she was tired, perhaps reading the words wrong. She searched more, found similar articles all proving the same thing.

Wherever Ivy had gone, it wasn't to the hotel.

Unless she chose an empty, dusty room to use as her final resting place.

Mariah tried to shove the thoughts away but they were persistent. She couldn't help but feel guilty. She'd been supportive of her sister but not overly so. She'd invited Ivy into her home for what was meant to be months, not years. She'd done the chores, bought the groceries, and supported her sister financially. Yet she hadn't done it for the right reasons. In the back of her mind, Scott had always been there, dripping with sweat and nibbling her neck. Their six nights together had stayed with her like a growth, some terminal lump she desperately needed to remove. It was the guilt that made her take Ivy in, not concern for her sister's well-being.

But none of that mattered now, she thought as she drove the rental (not a PT Cruiser but a Kia something-or-other that felt cheaply made and ready to fall apart) past the green sign that chilled her even worse than the newspaper article.

Not cute, she thought while reading the words. Or, more specifically, the words that hadn't been spray-painted over.

Last stop.

She drove for several minutes along a wooded road, telling herself this was all just a mix up. Ivy had gone away to a tropical island somewhere. She was sipping fruity cocktails and soaking up the sun instead of lying dead in an abandoned hotel.

Up ahead Marlowe came into view. It wasn't the ghost town she'd expected but it wasn't a raging metropolis either. There were cars parked along Main Street, the occasional shoppers stepping in and out of stores, but no one looked particularly happy. She wondered if those that had stayed behind would ever feel at home. How did you get over something like that? Did the teachers at Columbine ever feel safe again or did they look over their shoulders each morning before homeroom?

She spotted the hotel. It was hard to miss, standing much taller than every other structure in Marlowe. She parked, stepped outside, and shivered. The temperature hadn't been this cold at Logan. She was sure of it.

It was getting dark, the sun moving farther into the trees. She hurried toward the front door of the hotel, stepping under the marquee that reminded her of decades gone by. She moved quickly, didn't want to stick around come nightfall.

No, you don't get to run away because you're scared. Your sister—if she's even alive—needs you right now. Keep telling yourself you're strong if that's what it takes.

She stopped at the front doors and felt like crying. It came as no surprise they were boarded up. Some part of her had hoped the article was a prank. She tried to peer between the slats of wood but whoever sealed the place up had done a good job.

From her left, someone cleared their throat. Her heart jumped. She expected to see something inhuman, something with an impossibly large mouth filled with impossibly large teeth. Instead it was a short man with a bowtie. His hair was gray, thinning with age, and he reminded her of an English professor. "Can I help you, miss?"

She shook her head, then nodded. "Maybe you can. Is there another hotel in town?"

He smiled, as if she were playing a joke, then seemed to realize just how serious she was. "Afraid not. There was a bed and breakfast a few miles down the road. A woman by the name of Angie opened it. But as you can imagine, it didn't drum up a whole lot of business. She closed shop after a few months."

"Then where does someone stay if they come here? If they aren't *from* here."

He shrugged. "Nowhere. Miss, you do know where you are, right? This is—"

She held up her hands. "I'm well aware. It's just ... I'm supposed to meet someone here. I'm having trouble finding them."

"Quite an odd place to meet. Are you sure they didn't say Ipswich or Essex? Both are just down the road."

She winced against the migraine. She'd taken several Excedrin earlier. Her symptoms had lessened but they remained in the background, taunting her with each mile she traveled. "I'm positive. It's here, in this town, and she's missing."

"Who is?"

"My sister."

"Maybe she's just running late. Maybe she doesn't know the hotel's condemned and will probably be tore down if anyone gets around to caring."

She wanted to tell him he didn't know what he was talking

about. Her sister was inside those condemned walls this very moment, preparing to take her own life if she hadn't already. But she didn't have the heart to snap at the man. His eyes had a kindness she hadn't seen in quite some time. His smile allowed her to take her first deep breath since landing. "Did you know him?"

His smile contorted. "I'm guessing you mean the Ashton boy."

She nodded. "I didn't mean to touch a nerve. You probably get that a lot. I bet plenty of sickos come here, to the scene of the crime, asking all about what happened."

"You'd be surprised. There was some of that after it first happened but it's tapered off. The occasional ghost hunter travels through, searching for evil spirits but they always leave empty handed."

She looked into the distance. The sun was fading quickly. "No ghosts in Marlowe, huh?"

"I'm not sure I believe in ghosts but if they do exist, they'd be someplace like this, where something senseless happened to innocent people. But if I were a ghost, I wouldn't want to be bothered. I'd keep to myself."

"Yeah," she said. "Me too. I'm sorry I wasted your time. It's getting late and my eyes are closing."

"Not a bother at all." He patted her on the shoulder. The gesture reminded her of her grandmother, in the ground ten years now. No matter how hysterical Mariah had been, no matter how big of a fight she'd gotten into with Ivy, her grammy was able to calm her down with nothing more than a touch. "I hope you find what you're looking for. And I hope it's somewhere other than here."

"That makes two of us."

She made to leave but he held onto her arm. "I did know him. The Ashton boy, I mean. Not well but I knew him. I was running late that night. I work in the city. Traffic is a bitch if you'll excuse my French, especially driving somewhere so far out of the way. When I came home my door had been busted open. Nothing had been taken or destroyed. I didn't think anything of it at the time. Not until later that night when I heard the sirens. They were everywhere, in every direction, and they didn't stop for hours. Sometimes, when I can't sleep, I still hear those things. Or maybe it's just my ears ringing. I knew he was a bad seed. I just didn't know how bad until that night. I've thanked God for rush hour on more than one occasion and I haven't complained about traffic since."

The man looked at something behind Mariah. She was certain that if she turned, she wouldn't like the source of his interest. Then, as if his face had never looked worried, he was the cute, little English professor once more. All smiles and wisdom. He was good at hiding his fear. "Have a great evening."

He walked away, whistling some tune she couldn't place.

When he was gone, Mariah looked again at the boards sealing her from the hotel's interior, wondered if there was another way in, wondered if it was worth looking.

Wondered where the hell her sister had gone.

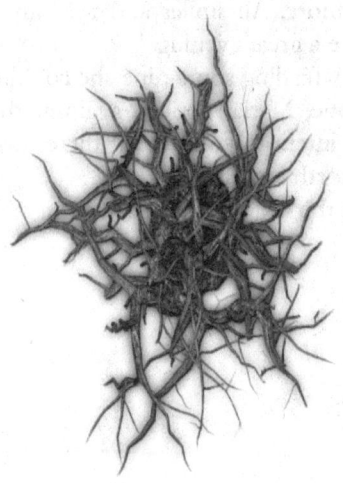

The following excerpts were taken from Charles Williamson's *Birth of a Monster*, published on the day of his death.

The night Tucker Ashton came back to Marlowe, it rained torrents into the streets. Several road crews had been called out to deal with flooding. A few streets were closed to traffic. The police were busy with calls of their own, as was the fire department. Basements had been ruined. Animals had been trapped. The residents of Marlowe recall the storm as a nightmare, though that is a term much more fitting for what happened next.

It is still unclear how long Tucker was in Marlowe before he went on his final—and most infamous—killing spree. Before his disappearance, he gave several different answers. First, he told officials it had been mere hours. Then it was days. Then even months (which does not add up with the timeline of his trip across the country). The reason for this discrepancy was not to confuse those that interviewed him. The reason, he claimed on more than one occasion, was simple.

He couldn't be certain. Time, according to Tucker Ashton,

moved differently in his hometown. He could not explain the phenomenon, yet he knew it to be true. One recurring theme during his many interrogations was the idea that Marlowe had called him back. He'd felt such an urge to return, he became sickly. Except when Tucker did return, he was let down. Some part of him believed the town would be different, changed somehow. He expected, no matter how irrational, to come home and be accepted, to be *noticed*. Never mind that, at this point, he was the nation's most wanted killer.

He went on record claiming he would "build his own Marlowe," his own version of the place into which he'd been born. There, he would be in control of everyone and everything. If there had been any doubts of Tucker having lost touch with reality, they were shattered.

The rain worked to Tucker's advantage that night. He did not believe in miracles until he saw the storm clouds hovering over the town. He moved quickly from victim to victim. Investigators still question if he truly worked alone. His actions were too precise. Surely a single man couldn't kill so many people within a few hours.

The first victim was a man named Terrence Hawkins. He was walking his dog several blocks away from his home on Peabody Street, visiting the closest mailbox to drop off his cable bill. Terrence would turn seventy-five the following week. He and technology did not get along well. Friends and family offered several times to help set him up with online banking but each time he refused.

His dog, a cocker spaniel with three legs, was the first to notice Tucker rushing them. The knife cut so deep and clean into Terrence's temple, the coroner believed his death was instant. Others would not be so lucky.

Next was Jacob Matheson, proprietor of Jacob's Pub, one of only two bars in town and the most popular by a landslide. Jacob was known to forget about carding quite often, which drew in teens from surrounding towns. It is also the place where Brad Ashton spent much of his time after Diana's death. Brad was, Jacob used to say, one of his biggest customers. That night, business was slow on account of the storm. When there hadn't been a patron in nearly a half hour, Jacob opened the back door and smoked a cigarette. According to his wife, he had been considering selling the pub and retiring. He rarely hired help and, as he reminded everyone who would listen, he was getting too old.

He did not hear Tucker enter the front door, despite the creaky floor. The rain was much too loud at that point. Nor did he hear Tucker as he stepped past the bathroom and office, past the kitchen, and lodged an axe (taken from the emergency case near the jukebox) into his back. His spine was severed instantly.

The third was a girl named Tanya Gomez. She was waiting for the bus, had stayed at school late that night. She was the head of the senior Spanish club and was nearly done planning their annual trip to Madrid. Her grades were flawless. She had been accepted to Stanford early, set to study medicine. She was found hours later with a slice from her sternum to pelvis, the wound reminiscent of an autopsy procedure. The rain washed much of her blood into a nearby sewer grate.

The third and fourth victims were Sasha and Michelle Clancy. They were not related, their mutual last names simply a coincidence. It was a running joke between the couple. If they ever got married—and according to their friends, they spoke of it often—they would save time and paperwork. They had pulled over once the storm grew worse, visibility poor, to put it lightly. Tucker opened the passenger side door and hauled Michelle to the curb. She was the driver in the relationship but had recently undergone surgery for webbed feet. Tucker did not use a weapon. He bashed her head to the ground several times before using his feet to stomp on her neck. Before Sasha could unbuckle, Tucker stepped back into the car, pushed her outside, and repeated the process.

Perhaps the most vicious death that night was Annabelle Perkins. She'd been working the front desk at Hotel Marlowe, the only hotel in town aside from a small, short-lived bed and breakfast. The hotel's generator began to malfunction because of the weather. The lights flickered. She called her manager and was told to reset the machinery. The controls were in a small shed several yards from the back of the hotel. On her way out she tripped and split her head open on the wet gravel. When she attempted to get back up, Tucker held her down with a foot, leaving his right hand free to pull her hair and his left hand to saw through her neck (using a knife taken from the hotel's kitchen) until she was decapitated.

Her head was never found.

The body count rose at an exponential rate. It is estimated that Tucker killed a resident of Marlowe every five minutes, which is why many believe he enlisted some sort of help, though he denied the claim.

He'd simply grown more efficient, he insisted.

Police were called in from several surrounding communities, as well as state officials. The FBI did not arrive on the scene until Tucker had been detained. He was found in the basement of his childhood home, after first visiting his mother's grave, where he left a single rose. It lay wilted and shriveled from the flooding.

Tucker would later admit he planned on killing his father, whom he blamed for his mother's death. He knew this to be irrational, that a random act of violence had ended her life, but he could not stare into Brad Ashton's face without seeing Diana's open casket, her face very much not at peace. Tucker was shocked to learn the house had been put on the market one month after he left Marlowe. His father moved to an apartment complex for low-income families. There he lived until his eventual stroke landed him in a nearby nursing and rehabilitation center.

He searched through the old home until finally venturing into the basement, the place where he'd spent so much time as a child. It was there his madness was born and nurtured and it was there he was found after taking so many lives. All his belongings had since been removed, aside from one item. It lay in the closet, in a particularly dark corner. A single potato. It had rotted beyond return, black and bruised and misshapen. It reminded Tucker of a tumor, yet he found it beautiful, felt compelled to hold it like a child, sit cross-legged on the moist carpet (the rain had seeped through two of the windows), and wait to be found.

He did not resist arrest when police arrived thirty minutes later. He held his hands out and smiled as he was cuffed and taken to the cruiser outside.

The rain continued to pour and Tucker's miracle storm clouds held steady over Marlowe.

NINETEEN

FOR A LONG time there was nothing. Blackness. Pure and simple. No corpses or killers, no blood or screaming. That was not to say Ivy Longwood felt safe in this void. If anything, she was on edge, uncertain if she was still alive or if she'd died back there, being dragged by a walking impossibility.

In the nothingness she fell forever. Vertigo surrounded her. It became obvious after a while. She'd fallen into the infinite crack surrounding Marlowe. She'd been taken from the others and tossed into a pit that was, she assumed, never-ending.

Of course it is, she thought. *Ethan tossed a rock in, remember? It didn't make a sound. Not a peep. It just kept on sinking into who knows where. There is no end to anything. Not this nightmare, not your grief, not even life.*

She supposed this could've been death itself. Oddly enough, she didn't often think on the subject, though it surrounded her on a daily basis. Ever since Scott and his damned ellipsis and the blood that was very much fake in the real world but very much real in this fake world, she'd tried not to think about what came after. Some part of her hoped, on those sleepless nights that so often visited her, she would see all of her lost loved ones again. It was a pleasant notion no matter how quickly it usually faded.

But now she knew for sure. Death was infinite. Death was forever falling toward something that never arrived.

The pit was warm at first, what she imagined hell to be like, but it grew cold, then frigid, until her face came alive with a prickling sensation. She opened her mouth and screamed.

And was shocked to hear her own voice, to see something other than infinite shadows. The light was blinding, like staring at the sun that had shunned this town. She thought she heard angels, wings flapping softly, but what she saw was more like a devil.

Inches away from her face lay a severed head, the wound dripping drops of dark blood onto the floor. The eyes were wide, staring, and the mouth curled into a mischievous smile. "Welcome back," the head said. "Feeling refreshed?" Annabelle giggled. She lifted her head upward and reattached it to her body.

Ivy swallowed. Her throat was bone dry. Her tongue was stuck to her teeth and it took every ounce of effort to move it.

Annabelle brought a hand to her chest in mock surprise. "Silly me! You must be dying of thirst. Here, have some water." She turned on what sounded like a faucet, filled a glass, and tossed it into Ivy's face. That accounted for the frigid sensation along her cheeks and chin.

Ivy opened her mouth, caught just enough liquid to manage a swallow. "Let me go."

Annabelle giggled again. "Let you go?" The voice did not match the girl. It was too high-pitched, too child-like, but she must have been nearly twenty, maybe older. "You're free to go whenever you want. Within reason, of course. You can go downstairs to the party but you can't *leave*. That's against the rules."

"Party?" Ivy searched her memories and retrieved the invitation hurled through the diner's window. "The party."

Annabelle nodded. "It should be starting any moment now. That's why I needed to wake you. Tucker will be awfully mad if you're late. You're one of the guests of honor. He likes you, you know. That's why he didn't kill you. That's why he offed your boyfriend instead. He knew it would drive you mad, that you'd eventually come here, to Marlowe, your new home. He likes the strong ones. They're a bigger challenge."

Ivy moved her hands, certain she was bound to the chair on which she sat but her wrists and ankles wiggled freely.

"Like I said." Annabelle lifted her head, tossed it in the air a few times. "You're free to go. In fact, we ought to go now if we want a good seat."

Ivy stood and nearly fell. Her legs were weak and shaky. The room spun. It wasn't the one she'd checked into earlier. This room was more of a suite, with a small kitchenette and living room. The bathroom in which she'd woken was twice the size of her own back home.

Correction. Back at your sister's *home. The place where you live rent-free and rarely contribute to anything.*

Mariah must have been worried sick, pacing the kitchen, drinking too many cups of her muddy coffee, hands shaking with each sip.

Fat chance of that. Tucker was right. Mariah is probably living it up. You've become more of a burden than a sister. Her life would be much better without you.

Annabelle watched her, tried to hide a smirk.

"Something funny?" Ivy tried to sound tough as she finally regained her balance but her voice was too hoarse, her lips trembling.

"It's nothing, really. You *are* strong. I can tell just by looking. Tucker wasn't kidding around. But what does it *matter* if you're strong? You're stuck here for the long run, and by that I mean eternity."

Ivy opened the mini-bar and grabbed a warm bottle of beer. She studied the label. PBR again. She smashed it against the neighboring safe. The glass shattered, spilling lukewarm foam onto her feet, which she saw now were encased in expensive looking heels. Her legs had been shaved (she didn't bother with landscaping her body these days; it wasn't as if anyone would be seeing her naked any time soon) and she wore a dress of some sort. Red and white polka dots, quirky yet fashionable.

She held the bottle like a knife and stepped back into the bathroom. In the mirror she saw a stranger. Her face was covered in makeup. Gone were her crow's feet and smoker's lines. Her skin was smooth to the point of perfection. She looked, dare she say, pretty. It reminded her of another life. One where she'd been in love. One where she'd been able to hold down a steady job without seeing blood at every turn.

"I hope you like it," Annabelle said. She'd tied her scarf back around her neck. Ivy noticed that she too wore a dress. It was hard to imagine what the girl had looked like alive, but she had likely attracted a good amount of attention with her body.

"Where are my clothes?" Ivy gritted her teeth, extended the bottle outward.

"Those old ratty things? I tossed them. Besides, you look beautiful. Wouldn't you agree?"

Ivy did not answer. Instead she walked carefully toward the exit. "Make one move and I'll …" She trailed off.

"And you'll what? Cut my head off?" Another giggle. "Bit late for that. You can only die and come back so many times. We should get going."

"The only place I'm going is out the front doors."

Annabelle rolled her eyes, a teenager frustrated with her mother. "You don't listen very well, do you?"

Ivy ignored her. She backed toward the door and, satisfied the girl would not make any sudden moves, she spun around, opened it.

And froze when she heard the music. It was distorted, out of tune, chaotic. It made every inch of her newly shaved legs come alive with bumps. The soundtrack reminded her of the circus. It was coming from downstairs.

The door to the television studio opened.

Amy was still certain this was an illusion. The room in which she sat really was just a janitor's closet. Her mind tried to rationalize her surroundings but her gut knew better. Nothing in Marlowe was an illusion, no matter how unnatural it may seem.

She sat on one of the bleachers, where earlier that night (or had it been yesterday?), she'd seen countless audience members cheering. Now the room lay empty.

Or it *had* been empty moments before.

Now a shape stepped forward, shadows covering its features.

That felt like a blessing. Amy didn't want to see whatever waited on the other side of the room or in the hall beyond. She wasn't sure her mind could handle any more horrors. She felt ready to come undone. Her pulse moved too quickly, hadn't slowed since they'd passed the town line.

She'd been awake for the journey back to the hotel. She'd seen everything in painful detail. Several dead people carried her from the PT Cruiser back to the hotel. These weren't your average zombies. They may have looked like walking corpses but they spoke with an intelligence, albeit with horribly contorted voices, that made her shiver. They were far from brain-dead. Once inside Hotel Marlowe, they brought her to a room on the third floor where she was stripped naked and tossed into a bathtub. Foam and suds threatened to spill over. The bubbles smelled rotten, as did the water. Beneath the white frothy surface, the liquid had a brown sheen to it. She felt anything but clean as they sponged her body. For a long time she suspected they would rape or drown her, perhaps in that order, but they were disinterested as they cleaned her every nook and cranny. After, they dried her, put on the gown she now wore, and brought her back to the studio. There she'd sat in silence. Until now.

The figure stepped closer so she could see some of its features. It was a man. He was tall and his skin did not look as decayed as the others. In fact he almost seemed ... alive.

"You look like you've seen a ghost."

The voice cut through her. She felt its knife-like point slicing as her mind recognized the owner. "No," she said, scooting back on the bleacher.

"Did you miss me?" Zeke stepped into the light. He was covered in a layer of sweat, his skin oily and slick. He wore an expensive looking suit that did not *suit* him in the least. Normally he wore horror movie and metal shirts. Always black. His hair had been trimmed and styled instead of spiked up like a porcupine. He was not the same man she'd spent the last year and a half with. "What do you think? You like my new look?"

"Let me go." She didn't mean to sound too desperate but her voice shook beyond her control. "Let me out of here."

"If you hadn't noticed, you're not tied up."

"Your friends threw me in here and locked the door behind them."

Zeke nodded. "We couldn't have you wandering off before the festivities began. Did you get my invitation?"

"You could've killed me." She touched the wound and winced. They'd put fresh gauze over it after her bath, though it didn't help much. It still bled plenty.

"I'm sorry about that. Sometimes I don't know my own strength. I saw you sitting there, looking so damned scared, and I couldn't help myself. I *like it* when you're scared. If we're being honest, it kind of turns me on."

"You're sick in the head. I was wrong about you. Your parents, your teachers, *everyone else* was right. You may have built an empire with your serial killer fan club but it wasn't harmless at all. It changed you somehow. Made you into a monster."

He snickered, wiped a tear of laughter from his eye. "Monster, huh? You have no idea." He lashed forward, a snake striking toward its prey. She pictured his tongue spilling from his mouth, long and slithering and forked, just before he extended his jaw much too far and bit her face off in one clean chomp. This close, she couldn't help but stare at his eyes. Except they still weren't *his eyes*. They belonged to Tucker Ashton.

He did not blink once. There was movement in the pupils, like something swam within them. "He's watching you now, Amy. This very moment, he's watching and waiting. He can't wait. This is his big day, after all."

She felt herself slipping again, more tears coming on. She fought the urge, didn't want to give him the satisfaction of seeing her cry. "Why a party?" She tried to look away but failed miserably.

He shook his head, grabbed her chin so she was forced to stare. "Not just any party. A reunion. And it all … starts … now!" He clapped his hands.

In response the door slid further open. Shapes shuffled inside the studio. Some she recognized from her detainment. Others were fresh faces, using the term lightly. All of them had been injured beyond repair. A severed limb here, a gouged wound there. Every one of them dead at the hands of Tucker Ashton, yet resurrected somehow in this place, this alternate town made from nightmares. The logic of it all hurt her head.

"Let's get going," Zeke said. "We've got such fun in store. The night is young."

The dead came for her. They lifted her into the air and carried her. Had she been at a rock concert, she would've just been crowd surfing toward the stage, toward the main act. Except in the here and now, the headliner was not going to play her favorite song. He had something much worse in mind.

From somewhere nearby she heard music.

TWENTY

THE MAN WITHOUT a jaw reached into Ethan's pants. Not *his* pants but the ones he'd been forced to wear after waking in the hotel. They'd taken his wallet, looked at it with a passing glance and transferred it to his new uniform, a suit very much like those he wore at his day job. At the time, he hadn't cared. In all likelihood he wasn't making it out of here alive. He had no use for credit cards or cash. But now, watching the corpse study the contents of his personal life, his gut wrenched.

Because there was more than just currency in there.

As if hearing Ethan's thoughts, the dead man stuck his bloated fingers into the wallet and pulled out a small paper square.

Ethan tried not to seem fazed but the idea of rotting hands touching something so personal, something so beautiful, was enough to make him tense in his seat.

The man noticed Ethan's reaction, studied the paper, then unfolded it. He cocked his head in confusion. Though he had no mouth, his train of thought was quite clear. *What is it?*

"It's nothing," Ethan said. "Just give it back to me. You have no use for a little girl's drawing."

Another cock of the head, his shredded flesh dangling in response. *A picture? From who?*

Ethan thought about playing the sympathy card, begging for the picture back, but something told him this thing couldn't be reasoned with. It no longer felt remorse. It no longer *felt*.

The dead man stared at the picture, studied its lines and curves. The longer he did so, the more soiled the image felt. Ethan thought back to the day his daughter had handed it to him. Princess Lisa, smiling as wide as her lips would allow, revealing the gaps where baby teeth had been extracted by way of string and creaky door. Smiling like nothing could make her frown, like nothing in the world could invade her magical kingdom.

How wrong she'd been. Dragons were quite real. Maybe not in the literal sense but metaphorical beasts lurked around every corner. One day you could have a happy, healthy girl and the next she was battling for her life. But Lisa was a fighter, as was her mother, and she'd do just fine without him.

But what about the money? Childcare is damned expensive these days, especially for single parents. They'll fall to pieces without you. You're the glue in this equation.

He tried to quiet his thoughts. If he was going to die, he'd like to do so with some semblance of dignity.

The dead man looked at Lisa's drawing for a moment longer before crumpling it into a ball and tossing it to the floor. Ethan screamed, reached for the paper, but it stuck to the man's shoe as he walked into the crowd.

Ethan shook, his hands forming fists. He opened his mouth to scream but the voices around him rose in unison, drowning out the sounds of a man who'd lost much more than a couple of stick figures.

After bathing and dressing him, he'd been led downstairs. Past the bar where he'd drank stale liquor. Past the front desk where he'd seen his first corpse of the night, into a large ballroom that seemed much too grand for the Hotel Marlowe. Several crystal chandeliers hung above him, on a ceiling that seemed higher than the building itself. More proof this town did not play by reality's rules. As if that wasn't already apparent.

All around him, Tucker's victims clapped and murmured amongst themselves, voices raspy and mostly incoherent from lack of use. In the corner of the room, next to a tray of what looked like moldy cheese and crackers, stood an old fashioned record player, the rusty speaker more like a cornucopia. The music was horribly distorted, the vinyl grooves played countless times before. It was something his grandmother would've listened to. If he closed his eyes he could imagine the frail woman sweeping her apartment and trying to dance despite the arthritis in just about every joint. Except that was a happy memory. This song sounded wrong, out of tune. He covered his ears but the melody—if you could call it that— traveled through his fingers.

The crowd's laughter and applause died down. They were drawn to the stage at the end of the room. It was perhaps two feet from the ground, large enough to fit three seats that resembled thrones.

The closest door to the stage, looking more fit for a castle with its ornate design, opened. A man stepped out. He would've been unrecognizable if it weren't for his eyes and the smirk that never seemed to leave his face. Zeke took a bow.

More applause, more shouting from the dead.

From behind Ethan, someone tapped his shoulder. He spun around and spotted Amy. She wore a gown and her eyes had been swollen shut from crying. He hugged her tightly. There was nothing romantic in the embrace. He just wanted to touch something that still had a pulse.

Another familiar face broke through the crowd, wearing another extravagant dress. Ivy looked ready to faint. Gone was her air of determination from earlier. "What the hell is this about?" she said, nodding toward the stage.

Ethan shook his head. "I'm not sure but if the invitation is to be trusted, it's a reunion."

Amy dabbed her eyes with the sleeve of her new outfit. "We need to get the hell out of here."

"It's useless." Ivy pointed toward the front lobby. "I checked every door. They won't budge."

Ethan thought of the hotel's floor plan. Surely there had to be a utility closet that *hadn't* been turned into a studio or some other impossibility. Which meant there could be a pair of wire cutters hanging around. "What kind of lock? Chain or combination?"

She shook her head. "There aren't any locks. They just won't budge. It's like they're frozen."

"Why am I not surprised?" Ethan loosened his tie, undid the top button of his shirt, and opened his mouth to speak.

His voice was cut off by the feedback from the microphone that had been placed on stage. It hissed for a few moments, the sound loud enough to bring a physical sensation to his eardrums. No one besides himself and the girls seemed to notice.

Zeke straightened the mike and adjusted it. "Thank you all for being here." He smirked, held in a laugh. "Not that you had any choice."

More unnatural laughter from the crowd. It sounded more like moaning.

"We have three very special guests with us this evening. Celebrities, if you will. One of them rarely does appearances anymore. I think you'll be pleasantly surprised. First up, let's give a hand for the man who created our king, our fearful leader, our one and only ruler. I'm talking about his old man, Mr. Brad Ashton."

The crowd thundered with applause at the mention of Tucker's father. The man next to Ethan, cheek busted open from who knew what, clapped so hard, one of his fingers bent too far backward. It dangled at an unnatural angle. He kept applauding, eyes staring lifelessly toward the stage.

The castle-like door opened again and a man in a wheelchair was pushed in front of the microphone. He looked nothing like his son but Brad Ashton seemed just as scared as the other three humans in the room.

The two dead men transferred Brad to one of three chairs on stage. He spotted Jacob in the crowd. The bartender had put on a new set of clothes, a suit that looked identical to the one Brad was forced to wear. The axe had torn through the back of the blazer and what looked like fresh blood seeped through the fabric. Did the dead bleed? Brad hadn't thought so. Not until tonight.

Listen to yourself. You sound bat shit crazy.

Except Brad had seen enough tonight to know this wasn't a nightmare. It had gone on much too long. He would've woken up by now. The same went for any doubt he was still alive. The fear he felt in his chest—not to mention the piss that threatened to soil his new pants—was more than enough proof. He'd never longed for the sterile white of the nursing home until that moment.

"So glad you could make it," Zeke said. He spoke with confidence to the crowd, buttering them up for what came next.

And what, exactly, did come next?

"Let's bring out our second guest, shall we?" Nods and claps from the audience. Brad tried not to stare at them for too long, lest his mind come even more unhinged than it already was.

The door opened again. Brad peered in but saw only darkness. It swirled like mist rising from the sea. When he'd been back there, he'd had the sensation he traveled further than was possible. The ballroom, if he remembered correctly, was near the rear of the hotel. There were only a few feet until you hit the back parking lot. But in that room, within the shifting shadows, they'd wheeled him along for what could've been miles. Which further proved one thing.

This was not the same Hotel Marlowe.

Something rustled. For a moment he thought there was a bat nearby, impossibly large, flapping its wings and preparing to sink its jagged fangs into his neck, but when he turned around there was just a tarp. Two more dead folks, a man missing his left arm and a woman with no eyes, carried something underneath the plastic lining. They struggled, nearly dropped it twice, before setting it onto the seat beside Brad.

Something smelled horrid. The scent permeated the air but only he reacted, the crowd oblivious. His stomach knotted. He hadn't eaten anything today unless you counted the tasteless black coffee they brought to his room this morning.

"What's this?" Zeke said, pacing the stage, pausing for dramatic effect. "Is there a person under there? Who could it be? They don't seem to be moving much, do they? No, their performance is, shall I say … a bit stiff."

The crowd giggled in unison. If he had an ounce of energy, he would've covered his ears, but every bit of reserve left his body when he realized who was beneath the tarp, sitting just inches away from him.

Reunion.

Hadn't that been the word that crazy bastard used?

Brad shook his head. "No. You can't. It's not right." His mouth was numb, his speech slurred more than usual. His meds were long overdue. He hadn't taken his morning or afternoon dose. His arteries protested. His heart slammed against his rib cage, wanting out of his chest cavity, as if it, too, knew what was coming.

The two dead assistants grabbed a section each of the tarp and prepared to pull it away.

"No," Brad said again. "Don't. Please."

"Don't be such a party pooper," Zeke said, his grin wide like a shark. "She's been waiting so very long for this."

The tarp was removed. A cloud of dust erupted into the air. Brad tried not to breathe. To do so would be blasphemous. But he couldn't help it. His lungs were old beyond his years. A lifetime of drinking and smoking left him winded, left him taking a deep breath after only a moment of holding it back. He coughed so hard he tasted blood but he couldn't stop shivering like a patient halfway through a psychotic episode.

He was breathing in his dead wife.

The dust settled and the room quieted as they took in Diana Ashton's presence. Like the others, she was dead, only permanently so. She wasn't speaking or breathing or moving in her seat. Her skin had long since rotted away, revealing the bones beneath. Even her skeleton showed signs of her attack. Parts of her interior had been gouged. He could see where her mugger had bashed her beautiful face against the pavement. Had she screamed for Brad that night? Had she begged the heavens for Brad to come to the rescue? He thought maybe she had but it hardly mattered now.

He felt himself come undone in that moment. It was worse than when he'd received the phone call in the middle of the night, worse than identifying the body, worse than locking away his son, worse than learning Tucker had become a cold-blooded killer. His pulse fluttered in uneven increments and he could sense another stroke coming on. This was The Big One, the attack to end all attacks. He welcomed it with every bit of his broken body.

He managed to lift his hands enough to cover his face but the tears were persistent. They crept through his fingers, slid down his hands. The crowd grew hysterical. He peeked at them, saw the way they laughed and pointed and teased. "Kill me," he said. "Just fucking kill me."

The door opened for the third and last time of the night. It screeched so that he thought for a moment Diana was screaming but when he looked she was still very much dead.

From behind he sensed another presence. The air grew cold. His hair grew rigid. Those drops of piss finally won the battle, trickling onto his thighs.

The crowd stood and pointed at something behind him. They looked equally shocked and mesmerized. It was the same stare blind followers gave their dictators.

A hand touched his shoulder and squeezed. A face appeared centimeters away from his own. A stranger's face. A monster's face. Tucker's face.

"Hey, Dad. Did you miss me?"

TWENTY-ONE

IT WAS ALL so beautiful. Being here like this, in Marlowe, in his hero's hometown—Zeke couldn't put into words the excitement he felt. It was almost sexual in nature. He could feel his cock stiffening as he watched Tucker make his entrance. So confident, every soul—or lack thereof—gave him their complete attention. Zeke had always wanted that, to not care what others thought. So what if his interests lay in the macabre? He hadn't been hurting anyone. He'd made a lucrative business out of killers, put himself through school, bought a house—had even been saving for a special kind of ring for Amy before they'd made the trip here.

Now, though, he wasn't married to anyone but Tucker. He had become, as if by some cosmic stroke of luck, Ashton's right hand man. He could sense Tucker's presence inside him. The moment he'd sat down in the studio everything had changed. Old memories vanished by the second. Even his time with Amy seemed distant. There was a sprinkle of affection left within his heart but soon that too would be deleted.

He looked at her now, craning his head away from the big show. She was crying. Always crying, that one. So sensitive. So weak. It didn't matter how hot she was, how good she could work her hips or tongue or how she made him feel when he smelled her hair and saw her smile. She was part of the past, would go the way of the other townsfolk before the night was through.

He smirked. This was Marlowe. The night was never through.

Tucker cleared his throat.

"I'm so glad you could make it, Dad." He bent forward as if talking to a child. "It's been so long. I bet you thought you'd never see me again. I bet you thought I was lying dead in a gutter somewhere. Or maybe *hoped* is a better word. Because we both know deep down inside, you always knew I was out there somewhere. As it turns out, I was closer than you thought."

Brad Ashton made to spit on his son but his stunted mouth worked against him. The loogie barely left his lips before it dripped down his chin.

"Allow me," Tucker said. He pulled from his pocket a handkerchief and dabbed the saliva. It was the color of tomato sauce. "Looks like you're bleeding. How fitting."

"Fuck you," Brad said. The words were barely a whisper.

Tucker nodded. "That's it. Let it all out."

"You're no son of mine. I didn't even want you in the first place. The only reason I agreed was because your mother was an angel."

"So *we* agree on something after all." They both looked at Diana and paused for a moment.

"Can't you cover her up?" Brad said. "Can't you use the last bit of decency you have left and put that tarp back on?"

"Why would I do a thing like that? Are you ashamed of her, Dad? Are you embarrassed of your poor, dead wife?"

"Don't talk about her that way. She was—"

"A great woman. Yeah, you already said that. But she died a long time ago and it sent you over the edge and you got nasty. You locked your son away in a basement. Your son who didn't have any friends, had nothing but time on his hands. But I made friends when I started killing. You know how many fans I have? People worship me, even if half of them think I'm dead. Even my victims love me. They have a way of coming back after they're gone. Kind of like me." He turned to the crowd. "Isn't that right?"

The crowd clapped and those who still had their feet stomped them onto the floor. It was deafening. Zeke was certain his ears would be ringing by the end of the night. It was worth it, though.

All of this was worth it.

Tucker turned back around, addressing his father again. "And you're no different. You wanted to get away from this town but some places don't let you leave. Some places suck you right back in. Haven't you figured it out yet? I have a gift. I made this place from scratch. All those nights in the basement, dreaming of killing—it turned me into something more than human. I kill and create at once. Once you die by my hands you get to live in this heavenly place forever. Would you like that, old man? Would you like to stand by my side for all eternity?"

Brad shook his head as best he could. A stain appeared beneath his crotch. Zeke smelled something foul but even piss and shit couldn't sour his mood. "Just kill me," Brad said, his lip trembling at an awkward angle.

Tucker leaned in closer. "You were never a good listener."

Tucker held up his hand. Zeke pulled the knife from his pocket. Tucker had placed it into his palms earlier, entrusting him with this important task. He handed it over.

Tucker wound back, held the knife in the air for a few long moments. "Let's be a happy family again."

Brad said something else but the words were lost in the blood gurgling out of his throat as Tucker brought the blade down, slicing it evenly across his father's neck. Red spilled forth in a small river. He convulsed for only a few seconds before he went still, though he wouldn't be for long. His eyes did not close in death. They remained open, unblinking.

Tucker licked the blade clean and the crowd applauded as if they'd never seen anything so miraculous.

Zeke couldn't agree more.

"We have to get out of here," Amy said for the fifth time.

Ivy agreed. She'd like nothing better than to bust through the doors and run like hell. But there was one simple problem. The doors were unmoving, sealed shut by some force beyond their comprehension. And even if they did make it past the doors, what then? They could run all they wanted, hide to their hearts' desire, but Tucker and his little fan club of victims would find them. It was a hopeless game of hide and seek and she wasn't certain if it was worth playing.

Perhaps it was better to give in, to let go.

Her opinion changed when Brad Ashton, dead moments ago, began to move again. At first Ivy thought the blade hadn't cut deep enough. The wound was superficial. He'd just fainted from the shock. But as she squinted and saw something that looked like a spinal column beneath the mess of blood, she knew she'd been wrong. He had been dead after all.

Emphasis on the *had*.

Now his eyes fluttered with movement, with understanding. His arms and legs wriggled like infant worms feeling out their new home.

"… not possible," Ethan was saying. "No way in hell. It's some magic trick. This whole thing is a charade."

Amy shook her head. "That's exactly the problem. It *is* real. All of it. Weren't you listening to what that bastard said about his gift?"

"I refuse to believe that." Ethan's tired face did not match his attire. The victims had shaved his cheeks. Gone was the five o'clock shadow but the bags under his eyes remained. If anything they'd grown darker and deeper.

"She's right," Ivy said. "It doesn't matter if you believe it or not. The fact of the matter is this: if that man kills you, you come back as one of his servants. Look around. That's what all this is. All these people were his victims. Now they're helping his cause."

Ethan rubbed his temples. Ivy could feel the headache from here. "And what exactly is his cause?"

Before she could answer, their attention was drawn elsewhere. Brad Ashton had stopped shaking. He surveyed the crowd, blinking like he was getting used to seeing for the first time.

"How do you feel?" Tucker said. He leaned in close, studied his father's eyes like he was a physician. He touched Brad's lips, pushed them around with the tips of his fingers. "Still numb?"

Brad's eyes widened. He shook his head. "No. I can … feel them." Then he did something so uncharacteristic Ivy's bladder shrank in response.

He smiled.

So that's how this ends. He kills you and you come back as his fucking employee. You smile and nod and do his bidding because you have no choice. He's the boss, after all. And Marlowe is on a hiring spree.

"See," Tucker said. "It's not so bad, is it? Death in Marlowe is a lot like life everywhere else. It's tough at first but you'll grow used to it. We all grow used to it eventually."

"What about me?" Zeke stepped forward. "When do I get to cross over?"

Tucker studied him like he was just a boy. He held a hand to Zeke's cheek. "I know this is difficult to understand, but I need you to stay human for the time being."

"But why?" He sounded on the verge of tears. "I want to be part of Marlowe."

"Don't be silly. You are part of Marlowe. The most *important* part. Unlike us, you can come and go as you please as long as I give the okay."

"But why would I want to do that? This is my home. I've been waiting my whole life for this."

"Because as long as you're alive, you can bring back new members of our township. Just like you did with Pops here. I may be the king of the castle but you're the prince. You're the *recruiter*. And business, as they say, is booming."

Zeke smiled. Understanding washed over his pale, sickly face. Ivy hated him then. He was just as bad as Tucker. She looked over to Amy and could feel the animosity flowing from her eyes. She'd finally stopped crying. Anger replaced sadness. It was a good look on her.

Tucker rubbed his hands together and licked his lips. He looked hungry. "Now, let's get on with it, shall we? If memory serves me, there are still three new hires that have yet to go through their initiation. Let's keep things moving. Who's up for a parade?"

More cheering. Ivy, Ethan, and Amy looked at each other, all of them just as confused, though all of them were sure of one thing.

Their deaths and eventual rebirths were right around the corner.

Then there were hands. Hundreds of hands grabbing onto them and turning them in the opposite direction. Leading them out of the ballroom, through the front lobby, and toward the magical doors that were, unsurprisingly, open again. Chilly air filtered in from outside and Ivy thought she saw something huge out front. Something monstrous.

Something starving.

But as they got closer, led by the dead folks around them, she saw it wasn't a beast but a float. A giant float of a dragon. It was crudely constructed, as if by a group of children. Its skin was dark green, the color of swamps and the things that dwelled within them. Artificial flames shot out of its bulbous nose, looking more like scalding magma. Its eyes were different from the rest of it. Whereas its body and face seemed almost comical, the two life-like orbs were anything but. They were a deep shade of red that reminded Ivy of the blood she'd seen so often back in the real world.

On top of the float were several seats.

"Son of a bitch." Ethan managed to stop for a moment, to fight against the hundred bodies behind them. "It's just like her drawing. It's exactly the same."

"What're you talking about?" Ivy tried to reach for him, touch his shoulder. It wouldn't help, she knew, but perhaps he'd be reminded they weren't alone tonight. They had each other.

"He got into my head and he made what I'm most afraid of."

The crowd behind them parted and Tucker stepped forward, slowly clapping. "Bravo. You've finally caught up to speed. I've been telling you as much all night. I *am* the dragon. This *place* is the dragon. No princesses allowed. When Lisa gets here she'll be nothing but a slave. I won't kill her, Ethan. She won't be so lucky. I'll keep her alive. All the progress she's made will be for nothing. Every cell in her body will get chomped on by those pesky little critters in her bloodstream. Because that's what dragons do. They burn you alive."

Ethan tried to break free. One of the dead smacked his nose in response.

Tucker stepped closer, took Ethan's face into his hand. For a split second, though it could have been a trick of Ivy's exhausted eyes, she thought Tucker looked like something else. Something that wasn't the least bit human. Then the moment passed and he was just a tall and skeletal man who made her want to faint. "It won't matter for you, Ethan. You won't care that your girl is suffering. You'll be reborn by then. You'll *like* watching her cry. You'll *smile* when she finally breathes her last breath."

Ethan growled, actually *growled* like some feral animal, and snapped his head forward, mouth open. He narrowly missed Tucker.

"You've got some fight in you yet. We could use more like you around here." He pointed to the ones holding him in place. "Load them up, will you?"

The dead did as they were told. One by one, the group was led onto the float. They sat near the front. Just above the dragon's face. Ivy leaned forward, peering at those red eyes. They were not made from papier-mâché. Whatever material it was, it shimmered with something moist.

They're real, she thought. *Those are real eyes and if you live to see the end of the night or the day or whatever fuck span of time this places goes by, the rest of the float will be flesh and bones. Nightmares come true here.*

The wheels began to turn. Below their feet an unseen motor whirred to life. She didn't see anyone driving, couldn't spot a steering wheel of any kind.

"Where are we going?" Zeke said as he stepped onto the float.

"I'm glad you asked," Tucker said. "I figured the graveyard is as good a place as any."

She did not hear Zeke's response but she could sense his grin.

The float picked up speed.

TWENTY-TWO

IN THE DISTANCE, Amy saw flames. She wasn't sure how far away the graveyard was. She'd never been good with things like that. It had taken four tries to get her driver's license. Her mother, as patient as could be expected, had gone over parallel parking countless times but the instructions wouldn't stick in Amy's mind. The mirror, she insisted, was one big lie. It showed you one distance but the truth was quite different.

"You just have to use your gut," her mother would answer each time, stepping on her imaginary brake as her daughter put the car in reverse.

"That's some advice," Amy would counter. "You should be an inspirational speaker." She winced now, years later, thinking how such talk must have hurt her mother. Or maybe she was being too hard on herself. She'd been a teenager after all.

"Mark my words," her mother had said. "When the time comes, when you get to be an adult and realize the mirror isn't the only thing lying, then you'll learn to trust your gut. And you'll think back to your old lady and say 'she was right after all.'"

"Snap out of it," Zeke said and just like that she was back in reality, if you could call this reality. She blinked and her mother was gone, just a corpse in a casket, the result of being in the wrong place at the wrong time. Another cliché, although not the least bit inspirational.

Her mother had been right, though, about what she'd said that day.

You did have to trust your gut once in a while. And if Amy's gut was to be trusted, she had to act quickly.

The flames drew closer and she could see there were three wooden structures that looked remarkably like funeral pyres.

It's too late to trust your gut. If you'd listened to her, you would've never come here in the first place. You would've never shacked up with a madman.

All around her, Marlowe came alive. Everything she'd sensed earlier, every creeping, crawling thing she'd imagined—all of them slithered in her peripherals. They passed an alley in which something large and misshapen crept. It had long, sharp fangs and even from her spot on the float she could see the saliva drip from its incisors.

On the other side, standing in the doorway of the post office, something made entirely of worms and slugs waved to her. The hand had three fingers, all of which came to points. All of which looked like knives.

These were nightmares, she realized. Impossible things come to life to cheer them on as they approached their burial ground. Though they wouldn't stay buried for long.

She tried to look away from the creatures in the street. Not that the dead people surrounding her were much better. She caught Zeke staring and smiling. "What's so funny?" she said.

He shook his head. "It's nothing really. I just like watching you, seeing you realize how wonderful this place is. I'm glad you're here."

"Makes one of us."

"Come on, it's not so bad. In fact, I'm jealous of you. Pretty soon you'll be part of this place forever. Imagine that."

"I'd rather not." She gulped, a plan forming in her head. Though *plan* was stretching out the word's definition. It was more of a last ditch effort. Not a solution but a way to even the odds if she played her cards right. She had to keep Zeke talking. "You really believe him?"

"Who, Tucker?" He shrugged. "About what?"

"His promise to let you be his glorified servant. Sure, you can come and go as he sees fit but what makes you think he won't get rid of you when you're not useful anymore?"

Zeke waved her off but she could tell he was rattled. "You've got to be kidding. If you hadn't noticed, he respects me, had me bring his own father back here. And the website? It's what gave him half his power. He appreciates all of it. Told me himself."

"Sure, he *told* you. But how do you know he's telling the truth?"

They both looked to the front of the float where Tucker stood, the ship's captain leading them toward a war, though it was more of a slaughter. The flames were close enough so they were reflected in his eyes, the same eyes Zeke had now. They were one in the same. Of course she didn't believe a word she was telling him. In all likelihood, Tucker was prepping him to be the next in line to rule this hell hole someday.

Zeke was staring at her again. "Can't you let me be happy for once?"

She snorted. "Happy? I thought *I* made you happy. We had a good thing going. Maybe your line of work gave me the creeps. Maybe I shivered every time I walked by your office. I used to call it 'the tomb' in my head. I wanted to make it into a joke if I met any friends at school but we both know how that turned out. Despite all of that, I never judged you like everyone else."

"That's not what you said back at the hotel. Sounded pretty high and mighty to me. What happened to everyone else being right about me?"

"Heat of the moment." She turned her head slightly so she caught Ethan and Ivy's attention. They'd been whispering every so often but mostly they looked defeated, heads hung low like prisoners on death row. She didn't mouth anything, couldn't take the risk. Instead she raised her elbow and pointed it toward Zeke, then pretended to stretch. They gave her a confused look but she'd at least piqued their interest.

"I did love you," Zeke said. "It may not seem like it now but I did. I still do."

"You just loved your work more."

"Don't be like that." He leaned in, touched her bare knee. The skirt of her dress was pulled back. She could feel the breeze on her panties. She did not like the sensation of Zeke's clammy skin, despised the way he glanced between her legs. But she could use it to her advantage. "We had some good times, didn't we?"

The worst part was that Zeke was right. They'd had plenty of good times. Picnics and movies and dates galore. All the things normal couples did. Except it had been a façade. Underneath their love, there had been something bubbling, something building toward the surface.

"Yeah, I guess we did."

"It doesn't have to end here, you know." He leaned closer. She could feel his warm breath on her ear, tickling the flesh. Once she would've been turned on. Now such things were unfathomable. "We can still be together."

That's it, she thought. *Lean closer.*

"There's something I've been meaning to tell you." She could smell his skin. It stank of sweat. She could almost taste the salty bitterness. "A secret of sorts."

His smirk grew mischievous. He thought she was flirting. She had him dangling by a string.

Or, better yet, a noose.

"I love secrets," Zeke said. He put his ear inches away from her mouth.

But her mouth went lower. She wanted one last line, something with bite, so to speak. Some satisfying conclusion to all of this. But she settled on silence.

She opened her mouth, sank her teeth into his neck, and clamped down. Blood poured onto her tongue, warm and coppery. She gagged but she did not let go until he pushed her away. A sizeable portion of his skin came away, his jugular exposed.

In his stare she saw something like hurt and knew he'd been telling the truth. No matter how psychotic and broken and vile he was inside, he truly did love her.

Tucker shouted something she couldn't make out. Whatever it was, he sounded frantic and angry. A horrible combination for a horrible man. No, not a man. She wasn't sure what he was now but he was far from human.

The dead moved in on her.

Zeke gurgled something but the words were lost in the red spilling from his mouth. His eyes changed. They went from a stranger's to the most familiar thing she'd ever known. His old eyes. His *true* eyes. Then they closed forever.

Amy turned back to Ivy and Ethan, nodded. She didn't need to tell them to run. Ivy started to move forward but Ethan pulled her back, mouthing something that could've been *thank you*. Moments later they were climbing down the opposite side of the float, taking advantage of the distraction.

Amy spit out the shredded flesh and swallowed, breathing freely, knowing she'd followed her mother's advice to a tee. She'd trusted her gut after all.

And in the end, though she'd lost her parents, grown estranged from friends and family, she'd found a *new* family in the worst possible scenario. She would not die alone.

The dead surrounded her, clawed at her, but she broke away long enough to rush to the edge of the float and dive head first toward the pavement. She soared for what must have been less than a second, though it felt like a lifetime. She struck the ground hard, her neck snapping and the rest of her body growing numb almost instantly.

Her last thought as she bled out was oddly wonderful.

She wasn't sure what came next but she was certain of one thing.

She would not be spending another night in Marlowe.

Ivy ran.

In the months after Brad's death, she'd grown weak and frail, had lost a fifth of her total body weight, but it hadn't been from eating healthy or exercising. Her diet was nearly nonexistent. Ramen noodles and leftover pizza. The occasional meatball sandwich when she managed enough energy to walk to the corner sandwich shop. She'd let her body, and perhaps her soul, fly away and now she suffered.

She nearly tripped several times over the heels she'd been made to wear. She stopped long enough to take them off and toss them into a nearby yard. They struck something hard and she swore she heard a grunt in response. Not a dog or cat but something much worse.

She no longer heard Ethan beside her. Perhaps he'd gone in a different direction. Splitting up was risky but it might work to their advantage. Or maybe he'd tripped somewhere along the way. Maybe he was being torn limb from limb this very moment. Would he scream during his final moments or would he die silently?

Speaking of final moments ...

She tried not to think of Amy. Just a girl. A sweet, innocent girl who'd chosen the wrong man. It happened to the best of them, Ivy thought. Usually it was abuse and infidelity, not being dragged into a nightmare city that defied all logic.

Her death must have been instant. You heard the thud when she dove off that thing. She couldn't have felt a thing. Stop worrying about her and focus on the task at hand. Make sure she didn't die for nothing.

But what *was* the task at hand? They'd already tried to escape. The gouge in the earth was surely still there, probably bigger now. She imagined it growing by the second so the mainland was just a tiny dot in the distance.

Footsteps from behind broke her train of thought. They were louder now, more measured, like Tucker's victims moved as one unit, with a single motive in mind.

To make sure Ivy's death was not as quick as Amy's.

To ensure she was reborn into the place she hated most.

Her legs grew weak and her feet stung. She could feel wetness on her toes, had stepped on something sharp. She couldn't run forever. Her lungs threatened to fail at any moment. If she was going to even survive the hour, she needed to find shelter.

She looked around. She was on a nondescript suburban street, the houses large but far from fancy. She imagined families grilling and playing catch in neatly trimmed yards. Now the grass was the color of ash and moved in patterns without the slightest hint of wind. She smelled something rotten, far from barbecue.

She picked a house at random, ran up the driveway. The front door would be locked, of course. Marlowe played by Tucker's rules and he would not allow her a hiding place. She took the steps two at a time, lunged for the door, and nearly cried with relief as the knob turned.

She stepped inside, into utter darkness, and slammed the door behind her. She felt around for locks and tightened them as she went, testing the door after they'd all been latched. It was far from sturdy but it might buy her some time.

The shadows were thick. She had the feeling things moved all around her, waiting for the opportune moment to take her into their grip. Tentacles and appendages and other slimy things filled her imagination. She touched a drawer, pulled it out, heard things shuffle. She felt around. There was a screwdriver, a handful of coins, and what felt like a notepad. A junk drawer like she had back in her bedroom. A place to store the things that didn't fit in elsewhere. Which meant there might be a—

Her heart skipped as her fingers wrapped around the lighter. It was the long kind, the sort of thing you'd use to light a candle or get the pilot going on the stove. There was something so normal about it, an everyday object that wasn't the least bit sinister. As silly and desperate as it seemed, she took it as a sign. Some small murmur of hope.

As she lifted it, her hand grazed something else, a rectangular cardboard box. It was crumpled, moist from condensation, but her pulse raced with excitement nonetheless.

She knew a pack of smokes when she touched one.

She opened the top, grabbed one of three cigarettes, and brought it to her mouth. She flicked the lighter. It protested at first, a car in the dead of winter, but eventually she got it going and lit the end. She breathed in. The filter tasted stale and sour. She wasn't certain how long they'd been sitting in that drawer—wasn't certain how time worked in this town—but despite the taste, it was the best drag she'd ever taken. Her lungs burned and she calmed long enough to at least consider gathering her thoughts.

She kept the lighter on, used the small flame as a guide. The windows were grimy, didn't let in the glow from the nearest street lamp. She risked a glance outside, sure she'd see a decaying face peering back but there was nothing. Her nerves still flowed with a warning. She felt watched from every possible angle.

She turned back around, tried to come up with a plan.

There is no plan. At least one of you is dead, probably two. You can hide out as long as you want but he'll find you. They all will.

She shone the light in the opposite direction. She stepped into the living room and glanced at the closest family portrait.

And blocked a scream from escaping her throat. The cigarette fell from her mouth to the floor, burning a small hole in the carpet.

These were not strangers in the photo. She recognized the father and mother from earlier that night, the latter now a rotting corpse.

The boy in between them, though—he was the one that blocked out her thoughts, replaced them with pure terror.

He was young, maybe ten or eleven, but even then there'd been something in his eyes, something about his crooked smile seemed inhuman.

Her hands shook beyond control. The photo, too, fell to the floor, landing face up. The glass cracked. The boy's smile grew more lop-sided. More horrid. He stared at her, features fractured, and she realized she'd chosen the worst possible shelter.

This was Tucker Ashton's home.

TWENTY-THREE

"NO WAY IN hell," Ethan said to no one in particular. At least he *hoped* no one heard him. He'd been running for ten, maybe twenty minutes, never daring to look back but certain just the same he was being followed. Eventually his right leg gave out and he tripped, landing on his elbow. The wound was superficial, just a scratch, but it still bled. He wiped it away, leaving behind smears on his arm.

When he dared to look behind him, he saw no dead people. Gone was the float with its fire-red eyes, not to mention the graveyard and its promise of death and beyond. He should've been reassured. He'd somehow managed to outrun them, losing Ivy in the process, but he was far from escaping.

When he took in his surroundings he realized he was at Fisher Park, the tiny, oval-shaped space where he and his childhood friends had played Frisbee so often. Memories came at him from every direction. His first successful bike ride sans training wheels. His first concussion from falling off said bike. His first trip to second and third base and nearly a home run on one drunken night after a school dance, though he and the girl—Shelly McDonald—had passed out before the deed could be finished.

He did not welcome these recollections, was in no mood for nostalgia. Yet they came uninvited.

His mind formed an innocent game of Frisbee, the same one he'd reminisced about earlier that night at the hotel. He'd been ten or eleven. It was a sunny day, nothing like the absolute darkness he'd endured since crossing the town line. His friends—Eddie Becker (now dead from a heroin overdose) and Todd Gardner (living out west and working for a radio station)—laughed and joked and it was almost a pleasant scene.

Almost.

In the distance, standing on the sidelines, a figure watched. It was tall and famished, bones threatening to burst through paper-thin skin. Its smile was not one of joy but knowledge. It knew something the boys did not, some joke beyond their comprehension, and they were the punch line. It was not the Tucker he remembered. His mind conjured a combination of memory and nightmare. The real Tucker had been tall, sure, and skinnier than most girls in his grade, but he hadn't looked so ghastly.

Hadn't looked so monstrous.

Ethan rubbed his aching legs, bent over and tried to catch his breath. He closed his eyes for a long time. The Frisbee game continued in his mind, neurons refusing to stop firing. When he opened them again, the scene faded. The sun was gone—and the stars, of course—and so were Eddie and Todd. But the figure remained.

And it was much closer now.

"What's this about?" Ethan said, trying to sound brave but failing miserably. "Are you going to give a long speech about how we should've included you more? How we should've invited you into our circle? Because that's bullshit. I talked to you in class. I was *nice* to you. And you know what? I'm sorry about your mom and your dad but you can't blame all of *this*, the killing and the torturing and the videos, on a shitty childhood. Everyone has a choice, Tucker. Even you."

The figure did not react, save for its lopsided smile growing wider.

For a moment, Ethan thought he heard footsteps. He spun around, doing his best not to lose Tucker in his periphery, but there was nothing. Despite that, he could sense something approaching. It could've been the parade of victims or something else. A sense of dread filled him, so overwhelming he thought he might vomit.

"Fuck this," he said before he jogged off.

For a while the scenery was normal. Everything was in the right place. He sped by Eddie's old house. The wraparound porch his parents had added was still there but it was badly dilapidated. Next door was the old candy store, still condemned, the wood splintered and charred from the fire, but it looked hundreds of years older than it should've been. If he kept in this direction, he'd end up near city hall.

Except when he turned the corner the scenery changed entirely. The houses vanished, as did any sign of businesses. Trees grew from nowhere and a lake appeared to his left.

He was back on River Road.

He stopped suddenly. The disorientation sent shivers through his skin. The world spun around him. He couldn't have traveled this far in such a short time, never mind the road was in the opposite direction.

Tucker was playing games with him.

Up ahead were the burnt remains of the stolen car. It still lay in the middle of the road. There was something sitting atop the front end, a small circular object he instantly recognized.

He wasn't sure how Lisa's crumpled picture had ended up here, miles from the hotel, but he did not question it. Instead he picked it up, uncrumpled it—

And nearly screamed.

It wasn't the same picture. It was still crudely drawn, as if by a child, but the scene was all wrong. It was the dragon that ruled the kingdom now. It sat atop the highest peak of a misshapen castle. The towers jutted at odd angles that reminded Ethan of a German Expressionist painting. In the background, mountains ran with tiny rivers of red. Blood, no doubt.

And in the foreground, the princess lay in pieces.

Her stick figure body had been torn apart and her severed head frowned at him, the dying eyes following his every move.

Above her head was a speech bubble. The message was too long to fit within the lines, let alone the page itself. Yet he read it just fine.

I wasn't brave at all, Daddy. The dragon was too powerful. It came while I was sleeping. I was so tired from the medicine and the doctor visits. I thought you would save me but I was wrong. Now I'm a dead princess and the kingdom is going to hell.

Ethan covered his mouth to hide his sobs. He knew it was Tucker messing with his mind, knew this wasn't the real version of Lisa's drawing, but that sense of dread he felt from earlier—it took him over. He felt like giving up. The ground called to him, seemed as comfortable as an aeropedic mattress. He could just lie down and give up and all of this would go away. The nightmare would be over.

From nearby someone snickered. He looked around, saw no one.

The laughter came again. It could've been inside his head.

"Don't be so silly," a voice said. "The nightmare is never over. Not in my town."

Something wriggled in Ethan's hands.

The drawing was gone, replaced with hundreds of centipedes. They crawled along his fingers and arms, explored his flesh. He tried to wipe them off but to no avail. They climbed and climbed until they were in his mouth and nose, invading his airways. He wasn't sure if this was real, if Tucker had conjured another hallucination or if this was where he died.

He closed his eyes as the things burrowed deeper into him.

The shattered photo was not the only portrait in Tucker Ashton's home.

The faint light cast a glow on the rest. There could've been hundreds, though Ivy was in no frame of mind to count them all. Many seemed to be taken by an unknown source. She couldn't prove this, of course, yet she knew it to be true.

The closest frame to her left, atop a busted fireplace mantle, showed Tucker as a young teenager, sitting at his desk and staring at something on the computer screen. It could've been taken by his mother or father, she reasoned, but some part of her was certain they hadn't been there when it was snapped. The angle didn't allow a view of the screen but whatever he watched fascinated him. His eyes were wide, his mouth curled partway between disgust and happiness. There was something erotic about the expression but something told her he wasn't watching porn.

She looked at another photo. This one of Tucker standing to the side during what looked like a middle school dance. His face was expressionless. No one noticed him. They danced and laughed without paying him any mind. That had been Tucker's greatest strength, she realized now, though she hated to give him credit for anything. He'd managed to go unnoticed for so long, to slip between the cracks during his childhood. And then when he *wanted* to be noticed, he'd turned into a psychopath.

She thought back to the book and her plane ride, how the author had glorified Tucker. Something clicked into place. The book and website and the videos—all of them gave Tucker power. Whatever had happened in this home, while he'd been hiding away, had changed him. Allowed him to feed off others' adoration of him.

She chose one last photo. Tucker was not in the frame, nor were his parents or anyone, for that matter. Instead there was a network of roots and branches, sitting in a mostly ripped plastic bag. It could have once been a potato but time and darkness had turned it into something else. She couldn't make sense of the image nor did she try, on account of the groaning sound to her right.

She spun around, nearly dropped the light. A door had opened. It promised shadows, the dark so absolute she could almost taste it.

And it tasted foul.

Ivy wasn't sure of the house's layout but she'd passed a set of stairs near the entrance. Those had led upward but these, she would bet, led in the opposite direction.

The basement.

Ivy knew what was down there. It was all in the book, after all. That's where Tucker had spent much of his childhood. Brad Ashton had locked him down there for days during his benders.

And now his father is a servant, reborn into Tucker's kingdom.

Ivy's sanity—what little of it remained—screamed with a warning. Whatever secret lay down there was best kept hidden. She was better off taking her chances outside, going house to house and biding her time.

Except that's *all* there was to do now. Bide her time and wait to be found. To be killed and *un*killed. The horde would not stop until she was back at the graveyard. And those flames? She was quite certain they could burn for all eternity if need be.

So why not go down those stairs, into who knew what? Why not face the shadows head on? When her mind conjured no better alternative, she held the lighter forward and walked toward the door.

On the first step she thought she heard something down there. Voices perhaps. Speaking in tongues, some dead language well beyond her knowledge. She pretended not to hear as she stepped down.

On the second step, she sensed movement. Something making its way through the basement with expert precision. Surely it had been down there for a long time. It knew its way around.

On the third step she felt something. It was the same sensation that came over her when she'd walked into her old apartment and knew something was wrong. The same gut punch she'd received moments before her life was eviscerated much like the man in her bathtub. The man she'd loved.

On the fourth step she decided to take them two at a time. Whatever waited down there would either kill her or not. There were only two options and she was too exhausted to decide which was more likely.

At the bottom her feet touched something wet. The floor felt spongy. When her eyes adjusted, she realized it was mold. Thick, sludge-like dew grew from the floor and walls. The room was perhaps the size of the kitchen above but that was where the similarities ended. Instead of a table and chairs, there was mold and must. The windows had been caked over with algae, the starless sky blocked from her view. Roots, just like in the photo upstairs, had grown through the floor. They covered almost every inch of the space. It felt like stepping into a tree's base, deep within the ground. Each vein seemed to point in the same direction. She followed their length. They ended in the left corner of the basement, where a desk and computer sat.

The screen was on.

It illuminated the space enough that she could turn off the lighter. She kept it in her hand just in case. The roots had formed over the monitor so the plastic casing was mostly hidden. The mouse pad had shriveled with moisture, the graphic forever lost.

The screen saver was a simple blue background that reminded her of the ocean, of better days gone by. It was hypnotizing. Her muscles relaxed, erasing their tender ache. Her mind cleared and she thought things might be okay if she stared into that deep shade of blue for the rest of her days.

Until the text appeared.

The keyboard was inches away from her, oddly unharmed from the moisture and mold, let alone the system of roots.

She did not want to read the note yet her eyes were drawn to it.

Would you like to know the Truth, Ivy? Y or N?

And because she had nowhere else to go—because she was all out of options—she leaned forward and clicked a single key.

Y.

TWENTY-FOUR

JUST AS ETHAN was accepting his death, the centipedes vanished, along with the choking sensation. He could breathe freely and breathe he did. Took in large gulps of air like they were his last. He didn't like the analogy but he was too busy regaining function of his body to care.

"Did you really think I'd make it that easy?" Tucker's voice was deafening. It came from every direction at once. Ethan spun around, tried to find the source but it was useless.

He was no longer at the river. The scene had changed once again. Each time he was transported, pieces of him came unraveled. His mind was not programmed for this sort of thing. It took a heavy toll on him and he wasn't sure how much longer he'd last.

He heard something nearby. He squinted until he realized where he'd been taken.

In the distance the gas station loomed. It was the most normal thing he'd ever seen. Inside, customers went about their daily business, blissfully ignorant how close to hell they shopped. The attendant read a magazine, flipped the pages without a care in the world. It was hard to imagine living like that. Such things seemed a lifetime away. Across the street from the store stood the sign, welcoming anyone who was dumb enough to pass into Marlowe, Massachusetts.

Last stop.

His mind did the math. If he was back here, this close to the gas station and town line, that meant—

He stopped himself from taking a step forward. The pit lay inches in front of him. His left foot was rooted to the ground. His right touched empty space. He stumbled back and landed on his elbows. Skin tore in protest but pain was the least of his worries.

He thought back to first discovering the gouge in the road, how he'd thrown a rock that hadn't landed. "It doesn't end," he said to himself, though he received an answer.

"You're starting to catch on." Tucker's voice again, omnipresent. It belonged to nothing and everything at once.

"Where does it go?" He thought about backing away but what good would it do? If Tucker wanted him to fall, he'd fall. There was no choice in the matter.

"Somewhere farther than you can imagine. Somewhere your mind can't begin to comprehend. Your brain would come bleeding out of your asshole if you even caught a glimpse. Wouldn't that be a sight? Too bad I don't have any cameras on me. That would make for a great video."

"So this is it?" Ethan looked around, tried to find something to defend himself with. Nothing but rocks and sticks. Besides, it wouldn't matter if he had a rocket launcher. There was no way to wound this man—this *thing*. In Marlowe, he was a god.

"I've had fun during your stay." The voice shook the ground beneath him. He could feel it in his teeth and bones. "We had some laughs, good times indeed, but I've got work to do. You know what they say about Rome and all that."

"But your commander in chief is dead. Not by your hand but a girl half his size. Which means he won't be coming back as one of your undead ass kissers."

"Yes," Tucker said. "That is unfortunate."

"How will you bring back new recruits? You needed Zeke more than the rest. You said so yourself."

Something moved in the pit. Whatever it was, it was massive enough to shake the earth. He sensed it climbing.

Tucker laughed. "Lucky for me, I've got my new right hand man cowering in front of me. Would you like that, Ethan? Wouldn't that be a cruel and ironic turn of events? If I let you live, only to do my bidding."

"I'd kill myself first."

"I thought you might say that but I have ways, Ethan. I have ways."

Ethan managed to stand up. He could see over the lip of the crack. There was something moving in the shadows, some shape seconds from emerging. He did not want to be anywhere near this place when the thing reached the surface. But running was no longer an option. Unless it was in the opposite direction.

"So what *are* my options?" He kept stepping back until he judged the distance to be twenty yards. He stretched his legs and ankles. It had been ages since he'd run a marathon—since he'd run at all—but it seemed as good a plan as any. Maybe he'd scale it, maybe not.

Most definitely not.

"I'll tell you what," Tucker said. "You can check behind doors number one and two but that's it. I'm not often a fair man but I do like to play games. Choose door number one and you can become my slave. Zeke 2.0, if you will. You'll require some extra training but I believe in investing in this town's future." Another laugh, knives being slowly sharpened.

Ethan nodded, ran in place. His pulse began to climb. Had the gap grown larger? "You already know my thoughts on that so tell me what's behind door number two."

"Someone's feeling adventurous. You want door number two? You're looking at it. You get to spend the rest of eternity falling toward the place you can't comprehend exists in the first place. I'll make sure you don't die, Ethan. I'll make sure you fall forever."

Ethan whistled, steadied himself. "Quite the decision."

"It sure is. Now which do you choose?"

"Neither. I choose to give you the middle finger and the get the hell out of this shit town."

Ethan sprinted. His legs protested from the start but he managed to gain some speed. He neared the pit, prepared to jump with every ounce of strength. Prepared to see Lisa again, no matter how impossible it seemed. For a time, he truly believed he'd scale the gap, that he'd make it back to reality after all. But he stopped at the last moment, just as the world shook more violently. Just as the object waiting beneath the surface finally emerged.

He fell once again, skinning his elbows further, though he didn't notice. His attention was drawn elsewhere. The thing before him, the thing climbing steadily out of the earth's core—it defied all logic. At first, Ethan couldn't make sense of its shape. His eyes burned and his brain ached just trying to process what he was looking at.

It seemed to have no form in particular. Or perhaps it changed every time he blinked. Hundreds of appendages clung to its every surface, wriggling and writhing on their own accord. At first he thought they were worms, more creepy crawlies to go with the centipedes from earlier, but the longer he stared the more he was able to come to a conclusion.

They were not worms. Or bugs of any kind for that matter.

They were limbs. Hundreds upon hundreds of limbs. Legs and arms and fingers and, he noted, severed heads. Its pattern was seemingly random and between the monstrosities there were stitches, keeping the flesh in place, keeping the dead at bay.

No, not dead. They were very much alive, he realized, as the thing climbed further out of its tomb. Every face contorted with pain, screamed with agony. It was deafening, yet he couldn't find the energy to cover his ears. The hands pointed toward him, reached for someone who could save them. The legs kicked frantically, as if hoping to detach from the mass in which they'd been attached.

He recognized some of the faces from earlier.

These were the true victims. The angry mob had been a façade. Tucker had granted them escape, at least for the night, but now they were back in their cage.

In the center of it all was a massive face. It did not resemble the dragon from Lisa's drawings but it embodied the evil she'd described. The thing was a cancer in and of itself. It was feasting on Marlowe, consuming everything it touched.

And it was within reaching distance of Ethan.

"What's the matter?" Tucker said from within his true form. "You're not scared, are you? Where's all that piss and vinegar from earlier?" Its breath was a thousand landfills, years of dead things left to rot.

Ethan dry heaved several times, and managed to get to his feet.

He turned around and headed back toward River Road.

From behind, the thing followed. Each step was an atom bomb detonating.

There was a loading screen. A small, nondescript bar appeared on the left and made its way to the right as whatever awaited Ivy prepared to install. The computer was oddly primitive. It reminded her of the one she'd had back in high school, when connecting to the Internet meant looking at simple websites and finding the occasional funny picture.

Every ounce of her body tingled. The air grew electric. She'd made a grave mistake. Whatever program was about to be unveiled was worse than anything she'd witnessed tonight. She'd never been more certain of anything in her life. This was Tucker's private sanctuary. It felt voyeuristic to be down here, like he hadn't yet realized she'd entered his home. But when he did, he would surely be angry.

The bar made its way across the screen slowly, as if taunting her. There was still time to leave, she told herself.

Her feet were growing numb. The moldy water on the floor had soaked through her shoes. The smell was getting to her. Breathing took great effort. She thought about turning around and climbing the steps but a small beeping sound broke her thoughts.

She looked back at the screen.

The bar had reached its destination.

The black screen vanished, replaced with a moving image. A video of some sort. The camera operator was far from professional as they maneuvered through what looked like a forest. Branches and leaves spun every which way. The audio quality was horrid. Wind assaulted the speakers, made the scene even more disorienting. The camera steadied long enough to focus on a woman. She had once been beautiful, with long, strawberry blond hair and a flawless complexion save for the blood that lined her cheeks and mouth. Her eyes were half-open. She said something indecipherable, then stared at whoever held the camera.

And screamed.

It echoed through the trees. Birds fled in response. She held up her hands as if to block something, begged for mercy, received no such thing.

From off screen something heavy came into frame. Ivy thought it was one of the frightened birds but it slowed long enough for her to recognize the object.

A rock, large and jagged and stained red.

The operator lifted it, lowered it again. The woman screamed, much quieter this time. The process was repeated several more times until her face lost its features, turned to a pile of ruined flesh, bone peeking from newly formed crevices. She stopped moving after that.

The camera turned around, focused on a face that was quite familiar by now.

Tucker smiled, breathed heavily, and turned the camera off.

Moments later, a new scene formed. It was a different location this time, some sort of factory in the background, but its theme was very much the same. Another victim, another weapon.

More screaming and pleading.

Ivy covered her eyes but it didn't help. The scene played in her mind as each video wound through her thoughts. She'd never watched any of Tucker's snuff films but she'd heard of their brutality. The reality was much worse.

Each shriek, each heavy thud that brought with it more blood, threatened her with unconsciousness. She could not faint down here, in this dark place, lest she wake up starring in her own video.

When she looked at the monitor again, it had changed somehow. Before, the plastic had been covered with roots. Now, the material morphed into something that looked a lot like skin. It was distinctly organic. Like a liver or an appendix or a—

A heart.

Gears worked inside her mind. This was the heart of Marlowe. The birthplace of a maniac. The monitor expanded and contracted, as if connected to unseen lungs, pumping life into the town, providing this nightmare place with all the blood it needed to keep existing.

But all hearts stopped beating eventually. No matter how strong, there was always an expiration date.

She balled her hands into tight fists.

Something touched her shoulder. It was cold and moist and leathery. She batted it away, thinking a rat had dropped from the ceiling. When she spun around, she saw the truth was infinitely worse.

One of the dead had managed to get inside. She hadn't seen this one among the crowds. Hadn't seen him since he'd still been alive. She held in a scream and managed to speak a single word.

"Scott?"

TWENTY-FIVE

ALL AROUND ETHAN, the ground caved in. With each step of the thing behind him, gaining by the second, the landscape disappeared into the abyss that awaited him. What had once been a circular canyon now turned into a sinkhole.

The mouths making up Tucker's true form screamed louder by the moment. They knew what was down there, in the never-ending shadows. Tucker laughed in response. It sounded like a million car crashes.

Ethan's mind swam with plans, each of them a dead end. This from the man who had thought he could scale the crack and make it back to the real world. This from the man who'd been tricked into coming here by way of a scumbag brother and a bag of stolen pills. He could run all he wanted. If he managed to make it across town, what then? It was just as sealed off as it was here. Where did that leave him?

Nowhere. That's where it leaves you.

He heard a tearing sound followed by a cool breeze. To his left, a tree landed in the road. He turned to the right, missed its jagged branches by centimeters. More shrapnel followed: chunks of concrete, ruined cars, what looked like the carcass of some long dead animal. Tucker's aim was getting better each time.

If these things did not bludgeon him in the next few moments, the screams would be his downfall. They were horribly out of tune yet formed a melody just the same. A symphony for the damned.

Ethan had been raised Catholic, had been given a very specific idea of what hell looked like. Flames and demons and billions of wails from those banished there, tortured for their sins for all eternity. He'd grown numb to the notion, had seen too many cheesy movies about exorcisms and satanic cults. Now, running from the devil himself, he realized that portrayal paled in comparison to the reality.

Marlowe was the real hell.

The cracks in the ground began to catch up to him. Fissures formed along his periphery. He swore he saw things clapping with joy as the sinkhole enveloped more and more of the landscape.

An opening formed a few feet in front of him. He tried to dodge it but was off by a fraction of a second. His foot caught and he went down hard. He felt the ground giving way. He rolled at the last moment and managed to avoid falling to his death.

Tucker slowed to a stop. "I'd hoped you would put up a fight. You're even more pathetic than I thought." His voice was barbed wire against Ethan's eardrums. He prayed to grow deaf, to be put out of his misery.

From beneath his bruised and broken body, he felt the ground shaking. His stomach lurched. It wouldn't be long now. Soon he would fall forever.

He closed his eyes, pictured a time before all this. It was nearly impossible to block out the sounds around him but he managed for a few moments. In those moments, he saw his family. He saw his wife, happy as could be that they'd brought a lovely little girl into the world. He'd been hesitant about having children, wasn't too keen on the idea of such responsibility, but when he'd laid eyes on his little Lisa, he'd known this tiny creature would be the love of his life.

He wanted those days back. Was willing to do whatever it took. If that meant ending all of this before he was thrust into the chasm below, then so be it. He'd die knowing that his wife and daughter loved him, no matter how stressed he'd been. No matter how many sleepless nights or angry outbursts. He'd done the best he could.

He felt the ground around him, caving in at an exponential rate. His hand touched something thin and sharp. A sliver of windshield from one of the cars Tucker had tossed. He held it up.

The thing that had been Tucker Ashton, the thing much worse than that skinny young man who'd turned to killing, giggled. "Quite the knife you've got there."

Ethan shook his head. "It's not for you."

He brought the glass to his throat. For a split second, Tucker looked concerned. It was strange to see such a ghastly face convey emotion.

Ethan pushed the glass deeper into his skin, prepared for the sting and the blood. Prepared for whatever came after.

He closed his eyes again and he was in Princess Lisa's kingdom, far away from this place.

This is it, Ivy thought. *This is the part in every bad horror film where the ghost or the slasher decides to fuck with the main character. Find a fear and exploit it. Usually a dead lover. Bring them back to life, stand them in front of the camera, and watch the hero perish.*

She'd always rolled her eyes at such scenes. You knew the dead person was just that—*dead*—and so did the main character. Yet they always seemed to fall for the charade just the same, delaying their escape so they became trapped or worse.

"It's bullshit," she'd say to Scott after such a movie would end.

"What do you mean?"

"I mean you wouldn't hesitate like that. You'd know enough to get the hell out of there. They're dead, so what's the point in thinking otherwise?"

"It's just a movie. You don't know what it would be like since it's not possible. Not something you'd ever be faced with. But mark my words, if you ever saw a dead loved one—take me, for example—your mind would come undone."

"Agree to disagree."

Ivy blinked and was back in the basement, cursing Scott for being right. Every inch of her body came alive with tingling and no matter how much she reasoned that this corpse standing before her was not the man she'd once loved—*still* loved—it was no use.

Real life was nothing like the movies.

It was much worse.

Scott tilted his head and reached for her.

For a moment, she too reached but then leapt as if she'd been about to touch something poisonous. It wasn't Scott, she reminded herself.

"What's the matter?" he said. "I thought you'd be happy to see me. Isn't that why you came to Marlowe?"

She shook her head. "I … I just wanted to get over you. I thought it might help. I was wrong."

He stepped closer. "Get over me? Why would you want to do a thing like that?" This close, with the computer's glare—still spinning through videos at random—she could see all of Scott's wounds. The slices from Tucker's blade were like mouths. The flesh had dried, gray and bloated and rotten. She imagined what lay inside those openings, wondered if his organs had shriveled to nothing. His face was the worst. He no longer resembled the man she'd met at a small private school in Oregon. He was just another corpse reborn at the hands of a madman.

"Where were you?" she said, backing away from him.

"What do you mean? I was here the whole time. In Marlowe. This is my home now. We can be together again. Don't you want that? We never have to be apart, not even for a second."

Her mind further unraveled at the sight of him but a small portion—infinitesimal really—called bullshit. "If you were here then why didn't you show yourself sooner?"

"I was nervous. I didn't know how you'd react. Didn't know if you'd want to see me again."

She shook her head. "You were a great man, Scott. The *best* man. You know I haven't washed the sheets since you died? They're yellow and stiff and disgusting but I can't bring myself to throw them in the wash because then the last bit of you will be gone. I miss you every day of my life. I see blood everywhere I go because I'm so traumatized. Or maybe that's part of this hellhole. Maybe that was its way of calling me."

He reached out with rotten fingers, bone peeking from within.

She recoiled, hit the computer. Screams still sounded, Tucker's victims being killed by the minute. "You were a caring man, a patient man, but you were a terrible liar."

"Come on, let's get out of here and go back to the graveyard. It's time for you to come home."

She pointed to the computer, still fleshy and bulbous like a heart. "Tucker was saving you as a last ditch effort. A secret weapon. He knew I wouldn't be able to turn you down, knew I'd lose my fucking mind—and that's saying something—if I saw you again. He senses me here, in his room, in his safe haven. This house is a rib cage, Scott. And this place is the heart. He knows I'm close to figuring out his one weakness."

"I don't know what you're talking about. Let's get out of here." His face was fighting off anger and worry. Two emotions the real Scott rarely showed.

She nodded. "I couldn't agree more."

She spun around, heard him break the act and leap for her but it was too late. Her hands were already reaching forth, grabbing onto the computer, and digging in. The mass was warm and sticky, like something left in the sun to spoil. There were no wires or circuit boards inside, only flesh. She gouged the screen with her fingers, tore away strips of it. The video faded. Another screen appeared in its place. Something that looked like the blue screen of death, the warning that popped up just before a system crash.

Scott grabbed her shoulders and squeezed but he was weak. With each new chunk torn away from the mainframe, he yelped as if his undead nerves were linked to a single database.

The world spun around her. Her hands were deep within the object now. It no longer resembled a computer—or a heart for that matter. It was an amorphous *thing* and it was losing its form by the second. Outside, houses and buildings toppled. The ground broke apart. The moldy floor shifted beneath her feet.

Marlowe, much like her mind, had finally come undone.

Scott shouted something, begged her to stop, but she'd stopped listening. He wasn't the same man. He'd died—for good—and if she never came to terms with that, so be it. As long as she took this place with her.

She closed her eyes, screamed with every last bit of energy, and dug further into the heart of this nightmare.

TWENTY-SIX

MARIAH LONGWOOD WAS out of ideas.

After sunset, after pacing in front of Hotel Marlowe for a full hour, she'd found a loose board and pried it away. She shivered as she stepped inside and searched its shadowed hallways, leaving no room behind. Most of the doors were unlocked, the rooms empty, and somehow that was worse, like no vagrants would even consider coming here. There was no evidence of bums or hobos, no evidence of life at all.

Wherever Ivy was, she wasn't here.

Her chest grew heavy at the possibilities. Her imagination spun like a film reel, showing her every worst-case scenario. Ivy hadn't even gotten on the plane. She'd killed herself in one of the bathroom stalls back at the airport. Or maybe she'd done it at Logan, just after landing. Maybe she'd gotten abducted at a rest stop along her journey. Maybe this very moment, she was tied up somewhere, in a stranger's basement, screaming for help, each plea unheard.

Defeated and desperate, Mariah went to the last place on her list. The place she'd dreaded the most after deciding to come to Marlowe. She took her time walking there, telling herself it was a lost cause, though truthfully she was just scared shitless.

She stopped in front of a nondescript house, looking much worse than the picture from killwithathrill.com. It had been uninhabited for many years. A house that oozed dread the moment you laid eyes on it.

The former Ashton residence.

Like the hotel, the windows and doors had been boarded up, but even from the street she could see it was a hack job. There were several spots where the wood had loosened. Like the house itself would never remain sealed.

Like it begged whoever was stupid enough to come here to step inside.

She checked her phone. Still no messages. She'd been using it as a flashlight and her battery had drained to ten percent. She wasn't sure how long it would last. In the distance, the sky was turning pink. Morning wasn't far off, though she didn't think much light would shine in that house, not even if she tore away every last board.

You can do this. You can step into that place, where a maniac was born and raised, and you can look through the rooms where he dreamt of killing. You can do this because you love your sister and she's been through more than anyone deserves. You owe her that much. You owe Scott that much.

She stepped through the yard. The grass had not been cut for a long time. She wasn't certain who was in charge, perhaps the city since the home had foreclosed, but she didn't blame them for hesitating to come here. The long blades reminded her of claws or teeth or both.

She forced herself to grow tunnel vision as she ascended the front steps, each of them creaking and moaning. She found the loosest of the boards and tore them away just as she'd done earlier. She looked back once, hoping for a cop car, but Marlowe was just as abandoned as ever.

She tossed the boards into a pile until the space was big enough to enter.

She stepped inside, holding her breath. Listening closely for anything that might have breathed. In her mind, every nook and cranny swam with life but it wasn't Ivy hiding in the shadows.

She checked the kitchen, the dining room. Nothing. They were decrepit, filled to the brim with dust. Her pulse sped, like she was being watched from every angle, but she saw no evidence.

In the living room, she was just about to climb the steps when a noise caught her attention. She spun around, certain something stood just behind her. The noise had not come from this floor or the one above.

It came from the door to her left.

The basement.

She shook her head. No way in hell. Ivy may have been sick, may have had a list of mental health issues, but she wasn't dumb enough to go down there.

Was she?

Mariah held in a gasp. She would never know for sure if she didn't check. And she wanted to *make sure* she never had to come here again. She touched the knob, cold like ice, and turned it. With the door open, she covered her nose against the smell of mold. She sensed a presence down there.

Whatever it was sounded large. She thought she heard it aspirating. Perhaps an animal had snuck through a broken window and was dying in the darkness. She steadied her hand, shining the pitiful light down the stairs. It lit only a few feet in front of her, did nothing for the shadows below.

She descended slowly, cursing herself for not bringing along a weapon. Surely there was something upstairs, a knife left behind or one of the broken boards. A rusty nail may not have been much but it was *something*. As it stood, she was totally, utterly unarmed.

She shook her head. She didn't intend on fighting anything off. She'd confirm what was down there and get the hell back up, slam the door behind her.

At the bottom, she slid the neck of her shirt over her mouth and nose. The basement was rancid. Her eyes stung. Her throat constricted.

And when she saw the thing on the floor, her heart stopped.

It was the approximate size and shape of a human. It writhed in the mold and dirt, covered in something thick. It reminded her of a life-sized worm, born moments ago. She backed away, her shirt coming down and exposing her mouth. The smell was too much. The *fear* was too much.

She spun around and lost her dinner onto the floor. She promised herself not to look again before going back upstairs. Surely this thing, whatever it was, would not hesitate to strike once it got its bearings.

But she looked anyway, perhaps by reflex, and she was glad she did.

The thing stopped thrashing. Some of the slime came loose, revealing a face.

It was not a worm after all.

It was Ivy and she was very much alive.

She keeled over, hacked, tried to catch her breath but failed. Mariah had been a lifeguard in her younger years, knew CPR well enough, though she was rusty these days. She did not want to put her mouth near the ooze that covered her sister but would do so without hesitation if need be. She was relieved to hear Ivy catching her breath enough to stand up.

"Who's there?" her sister said. Her eyes were plastered shut with slime.

Mariah didn't answer at first. She'd never been in shock, had never quite understood the term until that moment.

Ivy held her fists out, clenching the muscles in her tiny arms. She'd lost weight since leaving home. "Scott? Is that you again? Don't even think about it. I don't care what you say. I don't want to hear it. I'll tear your fucking eyes out if I have to."

Mariah covered her mouth. The tears were sudden and they had nothing to do with the stench in the basement.

Ivy moved closer, hands in a boxer's pose. "Tucker? You finally decided to show up? Maybe it wasn't enough to kill you but I hope it hurt like hell."

Mariah managed to clear her throat. She took off her jacket and stepped forward. "It's me, Sis. It's me."

Ivy froze. "Mariah?"

She nodded, forgot for a moment her sister couldn't see her. "Yes. Mariah."

Ivy shook her head. "That's not possible. How did you get here?"

"I drove down a never-ending road, past a shitty gas station and a bunch of dead trees."

"And you didn't see a big hole in the ground?"

Mariah tilted her head in confusion. "Not unless you count the potholes. I think I need an alignment thanks to this place."

Ivy seemed to consider this. She let her guard down for a moment before recoiling. "How do I know this is real? How do I know you're not really him?"

"Who, honey?"

"You know who. Prove to me you're not Tucker."

Mariah forced back a second wave of tears. Her sister was in rough shape, worse than when she'd set off for Marlowe. Coming here hadn't brought her any closer to closure. She tossed the jacket. "Wipe your eyes off and take a look at me."

She did so quickly, as if Mariah—or whoever she thought Mariah really was—would attack at any moment. She opened her eyes for the first time. Surveyed her surroundings like they were just a façade. "It's really you?"

Mariah nodded. Her lip quivered.

Ivy took another step back. "If it's really you, prove it. Tell me something only you could know. Something you couldn't have learned from that book."

"What book?"

"Tell me!"

Mariah winced at the sound of her sister's voice, rising to near hysteria. What could she say to prove who she was?

Now's your chance, she realized. *Now's your chance to come clean. Tell her about Scott. Tell her how you slept with the love of her life when they first started dating.*

She opened her mouth but stopped herself short. What good could come from a confession down here? She regretted her time with Scott but he'd chosen Ivy in the end. He'd told Mariah their last night together he truly loved her sister. He hadn't expected things to move so fast, hadn't met anyone that made him feel like that. Like he was the only person in the world.

"Your ring," Mariah finally said.

Ivy raised her eyebrows. "What about it?"

Mariah swallowed, cleared her throat. "You found it in Scott's bureau the day after he died. You didn't know he was going to propose. You'd been dropping hints left and right but you know how guys can be. A little slow on the uptake. You put it on and haven't taken it off since. Because you think if you *do* take it off, then you'll finally be over him. And no matter how much pain it brings, you never want to be over him."

Ivy dropped her pose. She came to Mariah, held her sister tightly. "It is you," she said over and over, in between sobs. "It is you."

Mariah's mind swam with a thousand questions but she couldn't bring herself to ask them. Not yet, at least.

For now, she was satisfied with their embrace.

They held each other for a long time, crying like infants in the basement where a killer was born. It didn't seem so terrifying anymore.

Ethan fell for an eternity.

As a child, he'd developed an irrational fear of heights. It came from nowhere. He'd been on several family vacations, had flown to Disneyland and Yellowstone without any problems. But one morning he woke up and was certain heights could and would kill him.

Eventually he'd gotten over the fear. It took a few trips to a therapist's office and a whole lot of coaxing from his parents. Now, though, as he fell into the never-ending abyss below Marlowe, he realized the fear had never really gone away. It stayed with him, hiding in some deep crevice of his mind, waiting for the opportune moment to rise to the surface again.

He'd been *right* to fear falling.

Because he'd be falling for the rest of his life and then some.

A deep rumble sounded in the distance. It grew closer. Perhaps some beast had followed him down. Tucker, changing forms once again. Worse than the pile of death and limbs topside. Ethan would beg for blindness but his tormentor would grant no such wish.

The rumble came closer.

Closer.

Until it was inches away from him. Until he opened his eyes and realized he wasn't falling after all. He'd landed in the middle of what looked like a rural highway.

An eighteen-wheeler was mere yards away, honking its horn. The driver screamed something silently from behind the windshield. It was much too late for him to swerve.

Before questioning where the hell he was, Ethan rolled to the left, off the road and down a small embankment. He landed in a pile of leaves. His limbs tingled with pins and needles but he managed to climb back up. The truck had stopped up ahead. The driver, a man with a long, shaggy beard not unlike a wizard, took his hat off and ran for Ethan. "Jesus, mister. Are you okay? I almost turned you into a pancake."

Ethan regained his breath enough to speak. "Where the hell are we?"

The driver looked him over, perhaps pinning him as a drunk or drifter. "You need an ambulance?"

Ethan rolled his eyes, growing impatient by the second. "Where are we?"

"Just outside of Marlowe, Massachusetts." He pointed to the convenience store Ethan hadn't noticed until now. The same one he'd passed some time ago. He couldn't remember how long it had been. Then he pointed to something in the opposite direction, just behind Ethan.

Ethan followed his line of sight and spotted the green road sign. The one that welcomed poor souls to Marlowe. The one that some wiseass graffiti artist had defaced.

Last stop.

Only this time, Ethan was on the right side of the words.

TWENTY-SEVEN

A FEW WEEKS later, after things had settled down some, Ethan agreed to meet Andrew at the Ipswich Sports Bar, the same place where he'd been talked into stealing a certain bag of pills. Andrew had been calling every day. At first he played the family card. He was worried about his brother, he insisted. There was nothing more to it than that. But as time went on, he dropped hints. Insinuations. What it came down to was simple really.

"Where are they, man?" Andrew looked left and right, as if they were being watched. Fat chance of that. A fight had nearly broken out in the corner, near the slot machine, when someone had mistaken the redhead choosing the next song for their girlfriend. An innocent slap to the ass had quickly turned to a violent situation. Everyone's attention was drawn that way. No one paid the two brothers any notice.

Ethan shrugged, looked around. "I don't know what you mean."

Andrew nibbled on his thumbnail. It had always been a nervous habit, one that had grown more pronounced with age. And with the nature of his line of work. Which was to say: criminal. "Don't give me that, okay? Don't you think I deserve an answer?"

Ethan drained the rest of his beer. It was his third in the last hour and he'd hoped it would calm him some, dull his nerves enough to get through this conversation.

The *final* conversation, he reminded himself. He didn't plan on speaking with his brother after tonight. This was a last supper of sorts, though Andrew hadn't gotten the memo.

"Are you even listening?"

"Unfortunately."

"Tell me where you hid the pills and we can be done with this. I've got guys on my ass over this. They want their money and, quite frankly, so do I. I'm real sorry what happened to you but you got out alive. So do me this one favor, will you? You owe me."

Beneath the table, Ethan's hands turned to fists. "Owe you?"

Andrew nodded. There was nothing theatrical about the gesture. He truly believed he'd done Ethan a favor, like his life would be better from here on.

"I was such an idiot to come here in the first place. I should've never let you talk me into it."

"It doesn't have to be that way. We can still make some money here."

Ethan's fists tightened. "You want the pills? Go get them yourself. They're on the second floor of the Hotel Marlowe. Room 203. Ask for Tucker Ashton. Tell them I sent you."

Andrew slammed his hands onto the table. His eyes grew wide and for the first time Ethan realized how desperate he was. "Cut the shit or I'm in *deep shit*. I can't go back to jail. I just can't."

"Not my problem." Ethan stood. "You call me again, if I hear from my wife or daughter that they heard your voice or saw your face, you'll be praying for jail."

He made to leave but Andrew stood and cut him off.

The near fight had died down. Several pairs of eyes darted toward them. "Get out of the way," Ethan said.

Andrew stepped closer. "Not until you tell me the truth."

Ethan wound back quickly. Andrew did not see the punch coming until it collided with his jaw and knocked him onto his ass. He landed on a neighboring table. A half-full glass of something pink and fruity fell onto him. The redhead from the jukebox howled with laughter.

"*That's* the truth," Ethan said.

He slammed a twenty-dollar bill onto the table and left without another word.

"Hey, honey?" Alexis said from inside.

"Be right in." Ethan sat on the porch, watching the sun fade into the distance. It had been exactly one month since he came back from Marlowe. It was hard to think of this as anything less than a second chance. He found himself taking in small details more and more. Like the way grass smelled after it had been freshly cut. Or the way his wife's voice made his heart beat faster.

"Someone's on the phone," she said. "Her name's Ivy something or other."

"Tell her I'll call her back." They'd spoken several times since that day, had been questioned countless times by authorities about the disappearance of Amy and Zeke and wanted to get their stories straight. Oddly enough, they hadn't even been linked together. Not yet, at least. He didn't mind talking to her about what happened. It even helped sometimes. After all, they'd nearly died together several times. He owed her his life, let alone a few long-winded phone calls. But tonight he didn't feel like discussing such things. He'd gotten back from his second job a half hour prior. He was tired and sore and he wanted to spend time with his family.

After a few moments, Alexis stepped outside. "You want to tell me who Ivy is?"

"She's one of my clients at the bank," he lied. "Nice lady but she asks a shit ton of questions. I'll call her back tomorrow. Chances are, she'll forget what she was asking in the first place."

"A client, huh? You're sure you're not cheating on me?"

He spun around, grabbed her, kissed her. "On you? I'd have to be a nut job."

"You *are* a nut job. *My* nut job."

He breathed in. "I smell lasagna."

"It was supposed to be a surprise."

"Let's eat then."

As she stepped back inside, Lisa came running out. "Daddy!"

He kneeled down and hugged her tightly. He did not want to let her go. If he had his way, he'd bring her to work all day long. Would listen to the knock-knock jokes she'd picked up at school and the punch lines she so often got wrong. Eventually she grew antsy, pushed him away, and handed him something. "I made you this. Sorry it took so long. I wanted to get it right."

It was nearly impossible to keep his composure when he studied the image. It was a replacement, of course. He'd lost the original back in Marlowe. Somehow that had been the worst. Not seeing so much death and pain. Not coming face to face with a killer he'd once known to be a quiet and troubled child. The worst was losing his little girl's drawing. The new image was better. She'd been working on her craft and if she kept up, he could see her as an illustrator someday. A famous cartoonist who drew comics that matched her knock-knock jokes.

"Do you like it?"

"I love it."

Her faced beamed. She pointed to the background, where the dragon had once threatened the kingdom. "Did you notice it's gone?"

"I did. How come? Don't tell me you were chicken."

She shook her head. "Nope. Because it *is* gone. That's what the doctors told me, remember? They said I'm going to be okay because I'm so tough. They don't call me Princess Lisa like you but they say I'm brave. I figured the castle could be safe now. It's a happy ending."

He stood and lifted her. "It certainly is. What do you say we eat?"

She nodded, kissed his cheek, and ran back into the house when he put her down.

Ethan folded the picture and placed it into his new wallet. He felt more secure when he put it back into his pocket. Like nothing could ever threaten him again. He was back home with his family. His daughter was getting better each day. Things were good.

But as he heard something step onto his lawn, he remembered threats never really went away. You could fight them off, perhaps win for a while, but they'd always be there. Waiting.

He was certain something stood in his front yard, though he did not look that way. It was useless. The moment he turned in that direction, he'd see the outline of something tall and skeletal. Then the image would vanish as if it had never been there in the first place.

He heard a rustling. The sound grew closer.

He chalked it up to the wind and stepped back inside, closing the door behind him.

Princess Lisa was waiting.

TWENTY-EIGHT

"ARE YOU SURE about this?" Mariah said as they waited for the moving truck. It was running a half hour late and she was certain this was a cosmic sign they should call it off.

"Positive. What did we say about you repeating yourself?" Ivy looked over the pile of things in the hallway and front lawn. She didn't have much. In fact, it would've been easier to use Mariah's Jeep. But, Ivy had reasoned, there was something more official about the rental. Like she couldn't have changed her mind even if she'd wanted to.

"And what did we say about you lying to me?" Mariah folded her arms in the hallway.

Ivy finally stopped. "I believe you asked me that already. A thousand times, if I remember correctly."

"You don't have to do this. You can stay here as long as you like."

Ivy grabbed her sister's shoulders and squeezed. "I know I can. And I appreciate it. It's just time, you know?"

Mariah nodded. "I know." She was surprised at how badly she wanted to cry. Her lip began to tremble. She turned away. She'd always appeared to be the braver of the two but after whatever had happened in that godforsaken town, it was obvious she no longer held that title.

She poured a cup of coffee in the kitchen and offered one to her sister.

Ivy shook her head.

"Are you sure? It's going to be a long day."

"You wanted me to tell you the truth, right?"

Mariah stopped her mug halfway to sipping it. She thought for a moment Ivy *had* changed her mind. She was going to stay behind. The house, much too big for one person, wouldn't become so lonely. Her sister's quiet, nightly sobbing, though stressful, was much more preferable to no sound at all.

Tell her. She deserves to know.

She shook her head as if she'd spoken the words aloud. Not yet. Maybe not ever.

"Your coffee sucks."

Mariah's eyes widened. "What?"

Ivy nodded. "That's right. I've never liked it. Tastes like motor oil with a bit of shit mixed in. Whenever you weren't looking, I'd toss it, get my own somewhere else—anywhere—so long as it wasn't that crap."

Mariah did cry then. The tears came quick and strong and they were impossible to hold back. She set her mug onto the kitchen counter. Ivy hugged her. "What's this about? I don't think I've ever seen you cry."

"I just care about you so damned much. I want you to be okay again."

"You and me both. And I will be. That's what all of this is about."

"I guess you're right." It wasn't the truth, of course. The truth was Ivy needed more time with her therapist, perhaps more medication. She needed a safe environment, one Mariah thought she could provide. She felt more like a mother than a sister. Despite what Ivy had told her—that she'd just traveled to Marlowe to deal with Scott's death, to finally face it—she didn't believe one word.

She wondered if she'd ever know what really happened.

In between sobs, something caught Mariah's eye.

Ivy still wore her engagement ring. It sparkled in the morning. "Did you wash it?"

"What?" Ivy said.

"The ring? Did you wash it?"

Ivy shook her head. "Not that I recall. The only things I washed were the dust bunnies under my bureau. And my sheets." She froze for a moment, as if she were about to say something profound, but the moment passed when the moving van pulled up out front. It honked its horn.

Ivy smiled. "That's me." She gathered another box of belongings, set it outside.

Mariah stood in her way before she could come back in. "Tell me something."

Ivy sighed and rolled her eyes. "What is it now?"

"Do you still see it?"

Ivy's eyes widened for a moment, so quick you would've missed it if you weren't looking. "See what?"

"Cut the shit. The blood, Sis. Do you still see the blood?"

Ivy looked around, studied her furniture, now dust free, and the last few boxes of clothes. "No," she said. "Not since I got back."

Mariah's eyes filled with tears again. "I'm going to miss you."

"Me too. Aside from your shitty coffee."

They hugged once more. Around them birds chirped and the moving crew laughed at something. Mariah didn't notice any of it.

She was too busy reminding herself Ivy had never been a good liar.

It was going on midnight by the time she finished unpacking. The apartment was small. The listing called it a two bedroom but that was using the term liberally. In truth, there was *one* bedroom the size of her car and another space that barely fit her two bookcases and a coffee table. It was cozy, though. Just enough space for one.

She looked around, tried to imagine herself living here. She wasn't sure for how long. A year, maybe. Just long enough to get herself back up and running.

From the kitchen, the teapot whistled.

She put down the box of books, shut the stove off, and poured her tea. She opened the fridge, reached for the milk, and gasped.

In the span of a second, the milk and the other bare essentials turned into something different. Flesh and bones lined the tray instead of condiments.

And that wasn't ketchup covering the door.

She closed her eyes, counted to ten, and opened them again just as her shrink had taught her. She'd thought it was bullshit at the time, but now, in her silent apartment with no one around to watch, she felt anything but foolish.

Everything was as it should be. The butter was butter. The mustard was mustard. For the moment, at least.

She poured her milk, took a sip, tried to slow her pulse.

The new job was three miles down the road. She'd taken another teaching position at a public school two and a half hours south of her sister's home. Close enough for weekend visits but far enough that Mariah couldn't check up on her daily. She needed space.

And time to think about her next move.

She knew she ought to ignore the urges but that was much easier said than accomplished.

The job was a miracle. After her not-so-subtle exit from her last position, she'd never expected to land another teaching gig. The new job's administration had taken pity but she was not above such things. She needed something to replenish her savings, not to mention keep her mind occupied for the time being.

Because the urge—it called to her every waking moment of every day. It had been there all along. When she'd first left Marlowe it was but a seed but since then it had grown into something more, something with roots. Something that grew in the dark.

She unpacked for another few hours, until her back ached and her clothes were soaked with sweat. Another couple boxes in the morning and she'd be done. Then it was time for groceries, clothes shopping, and her new job. Normal things that normal people did.

She caught her reflection in the mirror above her bed and could've laughed if she wasn't so scared and, to be honest, a bit excited.

The blood was back. It never stayed away for long. No matter how many breathing exercises, no matter how many times she told herself it wasn't real, just a by-product of grief.

It always came back.

It covered her now. More of her was red than tan. It stuck to her like a second skin, a *new* skin, which seemed fitting.

There, in her tiny bedroom, she felt it for the thousandth time since that night in Tucker Ashton's basement.

The Urge.

That's what all of this had been about, she knew now. The blood wasn't just calling her to Marlowe. It was preparing her. Tucker may have died that night—or maybe not. It made no difference. Ivy's fate was sealed.

Every town needed a mayor.

Every kingdom needed a ruler.

She closed her eyes and thought of all the possibilities, all the ways she could make someone scream and beg for mercy. She did not cry and she did not turn on her nightlight.

The darkness no longer scared her.

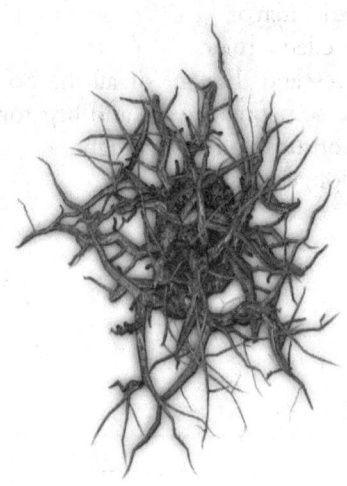

The following is a rejected epilogue to Charles Williamson's true crime book *Birth of a Monster.*

EDITOR'S NOTE: Charles, there's no way we can keep this in the book. It's entertaining, sure, insightful even—but just like the introduction, it reads as fiction. I suggest scrapping the epilogue altogether and ending the book where it really ends. Remember, this isn't a horror novel. It's reality.

There you have it. The life and times of the most notorious serial killer of the last decade. For many years, after what seemed like a gold rush of murder in the late eighties and early nineties, there was what many true crime enthusiasts refer to as a lull in activity. A crash, if you will.

Then came a boy who lived for the darkness. A boy who so desperately wanted attention he turned to torture, filming innocent victims during their most private moments. Their *last* moments. The lull officially ended.

Tucker's videos will live on. Many have been taken down by authorities but they always seem to make their way back to the surface. There are some things that cannot be killed.

And what of Tucker's fans? They are many. There are entire websites dedicated to the man's work. Take a moment now to search his name and you'll find countless forums and auctions. You could be the proud owner of his hat or glove or, if you're willing to dole out enough money, you could even have something from one of his victims. It's all out there, waiting for you, if you look hard enough.

A word of warning, though. Don't look for it. Don't even consider it. If you've read this far, it's already too late. It's still unclear where Tucker went, whether he's alive or dead but that hardly matters. His influence lives on, which makes him as alive as you or I. He's become immortal and his reach is far and wide.

Just like the potatoes in that moldy basement, his legacy grows by the day. His roots are strong and if you're foolish enough to go looking, they might just wrap themselves around you. Then you'll know where he went. Isn't it obvious? There may be no proof of any kind, no evidence he didn't die deep within the forest somewhere, but I've seen enough to know where he ended up.

Back to where it all started.

Back to Marlowe.

Back to the darkness.

Acknowledgments

Thanks to the fine folks at Grindhouse Press for being so darn awesome. See also: Emily Diana, Ryan Beauchamp, Max Linsky, Adam Cesare, Matt Serafini, Scott Cole, Matt Hayward, Aaron Dries, Matthew Bartlett, Tony Tremblay, Mike Lombardo, and a billion other people who've been much too kind to me over the years.

Acknowledgments

Patrick Lacey spends his night and weekends writing about things that make the general public uncomfortable. He lives in Massachusetts with his fiancee, his Pomeranian, his oversized cat, and his muse, who is likely trying to kill him. Stalk him on Facebook or follow him on Twitter (@patlacey).

Other Grindhouse Press Titles